Black Seraph

Library of Congress Control Number: 2006904765

To order additional copies, please contact us.
BookSurge, LLC
www.booksurge.com
I-866-308-6235
orders@booksurge.com

Black Seraph

A NOVEL

Sean David Morton
Wayne E. Haley

2006

Black Seraph

On the 2nd of April, 2005
An old man died in Rome,
With his death an oath was released
And this story then could be told.

CHAPTER ONE

"I had passed the old masque, the hour was near that of the crow and suddenly I was looking into the Face of Death."
A Thousand and One Arabian Nights.

March is always wet in Paris. The storms start at the top of the world around the Arctic Circle and then travel south by east. Scientists call this the Coriolis effect, and it steers the dense atmosphere with jet streams. Someplace over the high Atlantic off the coast of Scotland masses of moving air pick up great quantities of warm moisture from the Gulf Stream and through thermal conduction, this moisture forms large whitish-gray clouds that end up over France. Due to temperature inversion, warm air is always moving up in the atmosphere and collides with the cold clouds over Paris. During these periods, the sky opens and rain drops, the size of hen's eggs hit the ancient city with the vengeance of some prehistoric god who has decided on washing the gray city down the Seine River back to the sea.

The electric blue flash of lightning was punctuated by the explosion of thunder that echoed like primeval screams up and down the high streets and alleys of the section known as St. Clair. With each pyrotechnical display of nature and the ensuing sound of molecules trying to rapidly replace the vacuum that had just been created by the bolt of charged electricity, the rain fell heavier with the effect of attempting to drown anyone foolish enough to be outside during one of these storms.

Waiting in the alley for hours, and soaked to the skin from the rain, he never took his eyes off the third floor window where the lights had been on since early afternoon. The day had made its normal progress from evening into night and the ever-decreasing sounds of the city drifted away. His legs ached from standing so long but that did not matter. Thoughts of Knights Templar standing in the desert waiting to meet their ends a thousand years before he was born allowed him to push away personal feelings of discomfort. Role models of different times and places swirled around him in the alley, hanging like vapor and cobwebs.

The movement of the ordinary people had ebbed from a flow to a trickle on the boulevard, a hundred meters away from where he stood. Another flash of lightning illuminated the debris left in the wake of their passing. A brief pause followed, no more than five seconds, and the thunder reverberated off the ancient walls that formed the houses in this part of Paris. As if a part of the shadowed world he now blended with, Abdul pushed his hands deeper into the pockets of his black pea coat and leaned against the wall in the alcove where he had been standing for hours. For one brief moment he let himself go and closed his eyes, listening to the sound of the rain drops on the old cobble stones around him. It was as though he could see in his mind's eye the figure of Jean Val Jean carrying his daughter through these same streets trying to elude Javier in Hugo's masterpiece of Paris, Les Miserables. As a child, Abdul was frightened of the night, but now he knew only too well that it was his ally. He watched the movements at the various windows of the apartments above him with his peripheral vision in order to preserve his night vision. He hated Paris. It was old, dirty, and filled with the rubbish of human existence. He preferred the desert regions of the world that always seemed clean to him. Whatever telltale signs of man's presence arrived there were always quickly eradicated. This alley, much like the occupants of the shabby rooms above him, stunk of urine and the cheap wine bought earlier in the day at a flea market in Montmartre.

If he were caught tonight, he did not want to have on any clothing that would identify his real identity. No labels, watermarks, laundry marks, nothing that could be traced back to anywhere else. His fingerprints were not on file, anywhere. So if anything went wrong he only need keep his mouth shut and it would take authorities a long time - if not forever - to find out who he was. Abdul carried no identification on him of course, only a roll of euros, two spare clips and his semiautomatic pistol. If everything went right, in a few hours he would be back in his own clothes, sitting in the quiet bistro off rue St. Martin with a warm cup of coffee. He closed his eyes again and a slight smile of recognition crossed his face. That bistro is where he had gotten his nickname, Abdul, "Abdul the Bandit." Those that haunted the bistro called him that when he was not within earshot. He would come in, order his coffee and sit at the corner table by the window watching the comings and goings of the citizens of Paris. Seldom did Abdul speak and then only in quiet tones. The recluse never entered into the endless conversations about politics, finances, women, or the weather. So those that watched his comings and goings had joked that he was looking out the window for his next victim. They were closer to the truth than they would have wanted to believe.

His mind jerked back to the alley as an old tomcat slipping past the trashcans ten meters away made a sudden sound almost drowned out by the sound of the rain. Lightning flashed again. It took seconds for Abdul's eyes to readjust to the darkness and as he watched for movement, looking for any movement at all in the alley, he told himself again that he hated this place and the asshole he had to meet tonight, upstairs in one of those apartments. But this was the price for his sin, a lifetime of recompense for such a simple and human mistake. He tried to push the thoughts from his mind, but they were like leeches, sticking to him and sucking his life from him. This time the thunder was closer and louder. Abdul knew that most people would be inside, more afraid of the lightning and thunder than the rain. Early man believed that lightning and thunder were gods to be worshiped; they feared and worshiped that which they did not understand. The whole lecture came back to him. He could even remember the slides that he had used to augment the lecture, an Anthropology of Religion lecture he had given in what now to him seemed like some antediluvian period from another lifetime, before the creation of Abdul. Maybe it was another lifetime. Perhaps it was even someone else's life. He could no longer be sure. He tried again to push the thoughts away.

Her name was Jade and she had questioned him after the lecture. Was it really true that man worshiped all the things he didn't understand? He had suggested they sit in the student union and talk about it over a cup of coffee. She had insisted on her flat, an afternoon of give and take. She was a thirsty student seeking to suck the last drop of the professor's knowledge. He remembered her long raven hair falling across his naked chest, as she kissed him, the reluctant good-byes and then the lonely walk back to the rectory at the University. He pushed again against the memories, this time harder, that was another man's life, not his, not Abdul's.

Abdul looked up to the third floor of the apartment building. The rain was falling harder now and the lightning and thunder continued to attack the ancient stones of the city. He had to make sure that this slimy little character was not dealing with anyone else today. That is why he had spent six hours watching the activity in the rooms above him. There had been a lot of movement about four hours ago, but now it seemed as though everything had calmed down. If there were members of the security force or police up there, they sure were being composed. Not likely. But Abdul knew that trading in human flesh is the most common practice in the world. Selling out someone to authorities is still the easiest way to make money on the whole planet. From Ecuador to Algeria; it is always the same, give someone up to the local thugs in uniforms and you get a handful of yen, marks or rubles. Corrupt officials don't even care if someone has done something wrong. They use the opportunity to enhance the fear from which they get their power. Any junkie in the world; for a rubber cord, a needle and a bag of heroin, would sell their own mothers to the police, if they had a mother and knew where she was. This particular piece of human refuse he had to meet tonight was put together with spare parts from a department store that went out business because all of its merchandise was second rate or broken. What was he doing here again? This action had better be worth it! It had taken him months to set it up and now the pay off should start. Living like a shadow, avoiding all that was familiar to him and being the butt of jokes he hated were all part of the price. The danger of this operation he could handle, that was a given, but having to crawl through the sewers with scum like the man on the third floor went above and beyond in his mind. His mind drifted effortlessly through faces of men he had known well in the last ten years. But somehow, Amyl's had stuck with him. It had been in Morocco, where someone had given information to the secret police that Amyl was aiding some students that had become revolutionaries. The informant had earned the equivalent of five British pounds. Later Abdul learned that it had taken six days of screaming, in a basement cell, for Amyl to die in his own urine and blood. Just for trying to keep a bunch of kids from getting themselves killed. He had to stop this, stop thinking of the past. He was tired. He had been on planes back and forth through six time zones and then all the time he had spent today in this alley in the rain had drained him. The cold hours waiting in a standing position made him truly feel the lifetime of hatred that filled him.

Leaving the shelter of the doorway, Abdul moved swiftly to the outside iron staircase that led up to the third floor and Magre's apartment. Someone who had been expecting his arrival and was trained to listen for the minute differences in the environment might have detected his movement, but tonight the rain covered the sounds made by his shoes on the old rusted and worn steps. It was, for all intents and purposes, as if a shadow had simply moved across the alley. Carrying a full two hundred and twenty pounds of muscle on a six foot three frame, Abdul jostled through the window and stepped in the room.

The promenade had begun and now there was no one else on his dance card but Magre.

Magre sat at the begrimed table reading the tabloid. He was dirty with a four-day growth of hair on his face and charitably smelled like a farmer's hog pen. Magre turned after he heard the noise at the window. "My friend, Abdul, Abdul the Bandit."

"Shut up." Abdul looked into each of the other rooms. In one was a small water closet, fouled like the man, with urine and feces still in the toilet, and two or three torn and crumpled magazines littered the floor. In the bedroom lay a naked blond sprawled on the soiled sheets.

"Who's this?"

"A dead whore. She overdosed on some really rotten junk."

"Told anyone yet?"

"No, I was going to fuck her again, then drag her ass down to the alley and leave it for the dogs and winos." Magre smiled, showing his tobacco stained and rotting teeth.

"Why do they call you Abdul? You are not an Arab, or at least you don't look like a common sand nigger." Magre wiped his nose on the back of his arm. He put the tabloid down and picked up a glass of stale wine and made a slurping sound with his mouth.

"A true prince of a guy, Magre. That is what you are. The name — it is just that, a name, it's as good as any, you know, like Magre, the baby-raper."

Magre bowed at the waist enjoying what he thought was a compliment.

"You've got something for me?" Abdul pushed his tanned hands through his wet hair.

"Could be — then again I might give it to someone else. . . ." Magre smiled, rubbing his thumb and first finger together in the universally recognizable sign for money.

A large frame forty-five automatic slammed into the side of the Frenchman's head opening a gash that would take more than twenty stitches to close. He was bleeding like a butchered pig. "You son of a bitch, I will kill you!"

The speech attenuated when Magre looked into the barrel of the gun and then into Abdul's eyes. "You're a dumb bastard, who's got the gun and who is going to do the killing?"

"My friend, you are so angry all the time." With one hand holding his bleeding head, he started to get up from the floor where he had fallen. It didn't happen — a heavy Doc Martin smashed into his left knee and Magre fell back gripping his leg.

"For Christ sakes!" The scream came up from his gut and was mixed with a mouthful of pink-tinged vomit. It dribbled down his chin and into the gray hairs on his chest.

"Just lie there and bleed." Abdul tossed him a grimy dishcloth for his head. "You have something for me?"

"On the cabinet, between the books. . . there. . . yes, the envelope, it is for you from that old Jew in Warsaw. He does not pay me enough to deal with a crazy bastard like you." The towel Magre was holding to his head was rapidly turning crimson and his other hand clutched his knee, now completely numb.

Looking into the bedroom again, Abdul turned to the Frenchman.

"How old was she and where did she get the dope?"

"What does it matter - she is just another dead whore in a world of dead whores." Magre spit out the words like venom.

"It matters. How old?" The words were menacing, and the muzzle of the gun came up again, this time pointed at Magre's groin.

"She was what. . . sixteen, seventeen? What does it matter? She worked the corner and pushed her body in people's faces to get her fix and then she was happy for a while. Happiness in an unhappy world." His face was covered with his own blood and yet he smiled at his own joke. He started to crawl across the broken tiles of the kitchen floor so that he could lean against the wall for support.

"The dope, where did she get it. . . ?" Abdul stood above the man in a threatening fashion with the gun at his side.

"What. . . you don't care. I gave it to her. . . it was laced with strychnine. . . she was too dumb to know. . . ." He laughed. "I wasn't going to pay for that little tramp. . . she probably gave me a good dose of the clap anyway."

"There are worse things in life than a disease." Abdul looked down at the man, his eyes actually showing care in them.

"Like what?"

The lightning outside lit up the room again; three seconds later Magre's head exploded from the impact of the 220-grain slug traveling at 1100 feet per second. His depraved brain or what was left of it, painted the wall. . . the shot had matched the thunder exactly. . . one dead eye stared up at the man standing over him.

"Like dying and not knowing the rewards of a good life," replied Abdul. "At least you won't have to deal with me anymore."

Abdul walked into the bedroom, took a towel from beside the bed, and wiped the face of the young dead prostitute. He pulled the dirty needle from her arm, tossed it into the corner of the room, and closed her eyes. They had been intensely blue in life, but now had taken on the dullness that comes with death, in the moment when someone turned from a person into a cold dead thing. Abdul combed her hair, straightened her body in the bed, and covered her young white, once firm body with the sheet from the floor. Sitting down next to the bed he looked through her few belongings — lipstick, a comb, two stubs from the Metro, fifty euros, and a picture of herself in a flower dress standing by a river in a park. On the back was written her name, Nicole. . . he tossed her possessions on the floor again. It had been too long ago since he had known what to do at a time like this. There was a requirement and he was not fulfilling it. He closed his eyes and tried to remember the prayer that was needed, but the words drifted past him. They were but vapors now in his mind. Abdul raked through the embers of his soul to place a meaning on such a death as this, but it had been too long since the fire of understanding and belief had burned out.

He opened the letter from Abraham in Warsaw, though he knew what it would contain. There was a blue slip of paper with a number and a code word written on it in the small delicate hand of someone who spends their days writing passages from *The Torah*. This code would lead him to his "paymaster", one of a half dozen pinstriped bankers who were used throughout Europe for such business. These men knew nothing and cared less about the business that was being transacted. Only the fee mattered. The second card was white and it contained a post office number where something would be waiting for him; a key was taped to back of the card.

Abdul put both items in his jacket pocket and looked around the room that was a microcosm of a world filled with dirt, death, and the left-overs of decadence. Although not sure why, and certainly not wanting to explore the reasons for doing so, Abdul reached down and picked up the photo of the girl and slipped it in his jacket pocket too. Leaning down and stroking her hair with the back of his hand, he heard a few words drift up from him into the damp air of the room.

Abdul tugged at his collar and went back out through the window. It was raining harder and the night was getting colder. He walked west along the banks of the river. . . watching the shadows and trying not to think back.

CHAPTER TWO

"The worm of madness had crawled through his mind and
where there had been light, it left in its path only darkness,
which grips the throat of reason and tightens until nothing is left."
Diary of Gasam the Leper, 1248 A.D.

The Vatican is one of the smallest countries in the world. It is also one of the richest and in a covert fashion one of the most powerful. Encompassing only 108.7 acres in the heart of the city of Rome, it is properly known as The Holy See. The full time population fluctuates between 800 and a thousand souls. It is the last country on earth that still uses Latin as its official language. When the Kingdom of Italy was formed in 1861, the new king granted, or rather confined, the Pope's authority to the palaces of the Vatican and the Lateran in Rome and the Villa of Castel Gandolfo. All of this was guaranteed along with an allowance of $620,000 annually, but the Vatican has never claimed any of the allowance from any of the Italian governments.

In 1929 the Treaty of Conciliation created a concordat and financial convention between the church and Mussolini. Under the terms of the treaty, Pope guaranteed Mussolini that the Church would stay neutral in all political activities. In return, Mussolini gave the Vatican its independence from Italy and established it as a separate country. The ink was not dry on the documents before this pact was violated. In 1947 the Lateran Agreement, which grant further power to the men in the black robes, was incorporated the Constitution of the new democratic government of Italy. In the fall of 1947, the State Department of the Vatican established the first of various legations around the world under the title of Apostolic Nunciatures. Today the political representatives of the Pope represent the Vatican's interests in almost every country of the world. And on December 30, 1993, The Holy See and the State of Israel agreed to establish formal relations.

Just outside the boundaries on the Vatican in the city of Rome, thirteen buildings house the offices necessary for the management of this vast empire. They are protected and enjoy special extraterritorial rights. In essence, they are part of the Vatican and are untouchable by the local or national authorities within Italy. In one of these classic old buildings, just between the Viale Vaticano and the entrance to the St. Peter's Square resides the Office of the Special Congregation. In fact it occupies the whole building, all four floors and two levels of basements and connects to the Vatican Palace by an underground street which is lit twenty four hours a day and protected at both ends by a detail of the Swiss Guards. The sign in the lobby states that the Office of the Special Congregation was established in 1943 to aid persons displaced by the world war. Today its purpose is described in the small brochure, handed out by the young Jesuit at the front desk, as providing humanitarian aid for all those suffering in repressed or restrained conditions. Forty to fifty tourists a day stroll into the marble and glass entrance way and look at the Rafael painting on the wall, pick up a brochure and drop a few lire in the collection box next to the door. Few if any notice the ornate iron grillwork behind the receptionist which protects the stairway leading up into the building, all the way up to the fourth floor to the office of the Prefect of the Office of the Special Congregation, current occupied by the Archbishop Giovanni, the third most powerful man in the Vatican. With the exception of the Pope, the Holy College of Cardinals, those in the inner circle of power and the men that worked directly for him, no one else even knew that he existed. His power comes from the fact that he cannot be touched by anyone, with the exception of the Pope himself, and then only under the most dire of circumstances.

The Office of the Special Congregation was set up under Pope Pius XII during the dark days of World War II. To keep it free from the normal attacks of politically hungry Cardinals, Pius XII made it independent of control with the exception of the Pope himself and the director of Finance.

Once a man was named Prefect, the job was his until he died or became incapacitated with age.

The mandate given to the Prefect was simple — protect the Church. This simple statement had grown into an Intelligence organization that matched anything in Europe and rivaled the superpowers for its effectiveness and depth.

The Prefect's office was classic. Frescoes on the walls depicted maps of various regions of the world. Upon close examination, one might notice that the maps were as current as any Rand McNally atlas purchased at the local tourist office. But from afar, the way most people saw this office, they resembled 16th century maps with winds and compass roses and sea serpents. But that was, like everything else in this office, an illusion of a different reality.

The floor was covered in oriental carpets; the furniture was heavy, old and spoke of a kind of craftsmanship lost in a world of glass and chrome. The desk at the far end of the room was ten feet wide, sculptured from the darkest of mahogany. It was said to have taken ten workmen, sweating (but not swearing!) to get it into the room and into the position where the Archbishop wanted it.

It sat against the distant back wall, so that when the doors open and someone was ushered in, the man sitting behind that desk looked like an eastern potentate to be approached with extreme deference.

The room was extraordinary, but the man that occupied it was exceptional. Louis Gabriel Giovanni, Archbishop of the Roman Church, Prefect of the Office of the Special Congregation and Father General to the Order of the Militia de' Retainer of the Holy See was the head of the Vatican's Intelligence service. On a par with the head of MI 5 or the chief of the third directorate of the KGB, Giovanni ran all the covert and overt intelligence gathering operations for the Holy See. He also had oversight for the Gruppen Siben, a collection of special operatives to whom he assigned tasks that were more difficult to handle and that he felt priests should not take part in. Oversight — a word used to distance oneself from contamination. In this case oversight was a metaphor for being the principal handler of a large group of dangerous and deadly men.

Rumors abound in any organization — the church was no exception. In fact when you introduce selective celibacy and isolation from human companionship, rumors and gossip become the grease that coats the bearings of the community. The Vatican was a deck washed with rumors and many of them were about the Office, as it was known, and the lay brothers that wore roman collars and worked for Gruppen Siben. The truth was known to but a few and even they only knew bits and pieces. The complete picture was the property of the Archbishop alone.

Giovanni was 54 years old, with salt and pepper hair cropped short against his head. His olive skin was tanned, though no one knew how, since it seemed he was always in his office and never saw the light of day. Physically he looked like a boxer, a heavyweight. Large shoulders narrowed to a flat stomach and moderate hips.

But two other features struck people most often. His hands, large and muscular like a bricklayer's or stonemason's, did not seem to fit a man of the church. And his steel-gray eyes were penetrating, always watching, and though his mouth smiled, his eyes never did.

He had worked in the Office of the Special Congregation for exactly thirty years. He was 24 when he was transferred from his post in the Berlin diplomatic office of the Vatican.

He had known that someone had marked him for advancement years before this. He was studying to become a parish priest at a small theological seminary near his home in northern Italy, when two fathers from Rome showed up at the school. They spoke for hours to the Provost and then spent two days asking Giovanni hundreds of questions, none of which pertained to religion. At the conclusion of the interview, he was told to pack his belongings and was escorted to the train station and seated in a first class carriage with a ticket to Rome and an appointment to the Vatican University to finish his education. After graduation and ordination he went on to the International School of Foreign Affairs for a Masters Degree. He received an assignment to the Diplomatic Office of the Vatican and was assigned to Berlin. He had been there six weeks when he received the large buff colored envelope bearing the Papal seal and instructions to report to the Office of the Special Congregation, immediately. At age 24, he walked through the front doors of brick building not even knowing what the OSC was. In time he learned, and with great appreciation, he came to understand the power the OSC carried and how it wielded the power behind the Throne of Peter.

There had been three heads of the OSC since its inception. Each had served as apprentice to the director before him. Each man had seen others in the same role, but through a lack of understanding or an error in judgment those others had failed to complete the course of study necessary to assume the role as head of the OSC. At one point, Giovanni had thought that even he had failed and was about to be ousted, but he craftily placed responsibility for the error elsewhere, and then with only a moment of remorse watched as another neophyte exited the community to return to the world of masses, confessions, and the totally boring everyday life of a parish priest.

With skill and adroitness he had moved ever so carefully through the mazes and mine fields that characterized the bureaucracy of the OSC until he finally gained the attention of the director. He was called upon to suspend his other activities and received an office on the fourth floor across the hall from the office he now occupies. His first few weeks on the fourth floor were the most eye opening, jolting and at times revolting, of his entire life.

Father Giovanni was introduced to the true power of the Office and how it was used. Most ancient institutions have methods and ways of testing their younger members. The OSC was no exception. Before the large picture could be shown, a smaller sketch is given and then the reaction of the novice is noted. By bits and pieces the story was revealed and then a transformation occurred. With each compromise and each lesson learned, the novice commits himself to deeper acts of deception and duplicity, thereby learning the craft and by default or choice, compromising himself to the point where he can never turn back. His obedience and devotion to the Office outweighs all else because of the fear of someone finding out what he has done. It is a time-honored, simple way for an organization to build an agent to do its bidding without question. It depends on trickery, compromise, duplicity and fear of being revealed, all of which are not very high on the list of virtues in most theologies.

Within the OSC building there were places that even a member of the fourth floor staff could not go, chief among them the second basement. That level housed the records and files of the organization, behind an electrified fence, that had every modern security measure anyone had come up with, and then some that the German engineers that designed it added for good measure. Ten tons of strategically placed high explosives would reduce the first and second floors of the building to rubble as well as completely destroy all the records, files and incriminating documents which the OSC held in the basement. Only three men knew the destruct code and that code would not work without the key that hung around Giovanni's neck. His carried the ultimate responsibility. If OSC security was compromised to the point where someone might gain access to the storage in the second basement, he had to throw up the final defense.

The OSC was a special world and everyone in that world knew it. First, to be selected was an honor. Turn such an honor down, and one's career in the church went no place else. Accept the appointment and make it over the first few hurdles, and one would be offered a lifetime of challenges to protect the church's interest in every area of the world, through "non-traditional" methods. The reports that filtered out of the OSC spoke of the protection provided to liberation theologians, secular apologists and detained pastors in oppressed environments. Ninety percent of the work done by OSC was in the church's interest and indeed fulfilled the mandate given so many years ago. But the other ten percent concerned Archbishop Giovanni the most.

His old office space across the hall was presently the haunts of his two assistants, Fathers Marcus and Anthony, both Jesuits and both brilliant. Marcus was middle aged, tall and strong, with a handsome Roman face. He had worked for Giovanni for ten years and still had not learned all the ins and outs of the department. He dressed in the finest of suits, handmade in a little shop in the center of Rome. He didn't stay in the community in the evenings because he had his own apartment off the Via Roma overlooking the city lights.

He said he needed the isolation to work on the manuscript that he was writing. Giovanni knew the truth and was fascinated by it. Marcus lived with a lovely twenty-eight year old mistress, surrounded by the plush world of a high-rise building. She wore the latest fashions and vacationed in North Africa. That Marcus was twenty-five years her senior did not matter. He paid for everything and she had but one function, and in Giovanni's mind, she must perform that one function with great skill. Giovanni hated Marcus, not because of his family wealth, his lifestyle, or his mistress, for those were indulgences that Giovanni could forgive anyone. It was the fact that Marcus was so sure that he would replace Giovanni as head of the OSC one day. Giovanni was already laying the plans for the sacking of that particular Troy. Marcus would never sit in this room, behind this desk, or wear this key around his neck.

On this gray morning, Marcus sat in one of the chairs opposite Giovanni's huge desk. In the other chair, apparently intent on studying the pattern of the oriental carpet was Father Anthony, young, bright and handpicked to work inside OSC by forces outside the Vatican hierarchy. He possessed an MBA and was a Political Science graduate first, a priest second, and a computer nerd third. They had improved his looks with the contact lenses, the hair cut and drugs for his acne on his face. But Giovanni had wondered why he had been selected to one of the highest positions in the OSC, until the kid opened his mouth and started to talk. Then everything came clear. This young man had a complete handle on the stock markets on three continents. His ability to move money and make money was nothing less than phenomenal. He sat for hours at the three computers in his office. Sifting through mounds of information and then moving assets from one OSC account to another through some stock maneuver which would yield ten to fifteen million U. S. dollars in four or five hours of exchanging.

Then he would go back to reading the screens on his computer and watching for whatever it was that gave him the first clue. Giovanni had no illusions about this man's role. It was to strengthen the relationship between OSC and the men on the outside that had built the organization into one of power and wealth. He was their inside man, not Giovanni's, and as such, he was untouchable. But during the three years he had been there, Giovanni had learned to listen to him and trust in his judgment. He was astute and accurate — if not personable. He was young and smart and probably their pick to replace Giovanni when the time came, but that was not for some time yet, or at least Giovanni hoped that was the case.

Giovanni had re-read the file in front of him three times this morning. He knew the players in the file, but not to the extent that he desired at this point. Giovanni was aware that two of four the people named in this file had worked for OSC before and had completed their tasks well. The third was unknown to him, a contact in Saddam Hussein's governmental structure that probably wanted to remain in the shadows, or as they say in spy craft "on the edge of darkness". But it was the fourth name in the file and the short biography that bothered him the most. This man had come and gone for the past year and a half providing the OSC with valuable information and services, and yet no one could obtain very much information about him. Giovanni considered the reasons that a man live in the kind of world where lies, deception and betrayal were virtues. He looked out of his windows into the slate gray sky that threatened rain and smiled to himself. He knew the causes only to well, for they had been the same that had brought him to the seat of power that he now enjoyed.

Giovanni was more concerned about this present incident than he would like to admit. It could cause unwanted problems for his community and the church as a whole if things went wrong, and it did seem as though things had gone wrong. He looked at the memo that Father Marcus had brought in with him and then looked up to meet the other man's eyes.

"What does it mean that you can't find him?" The Archbishop was standing looking down at the file again. He spoke in a natural tone, trying not to alert either of the two men to his unease.

"We have tried all the known places, his contact points, his apartment, the library. . . he is not at any of them." Father Marcus did not look away; he looked directly at the Archbishop, meeting his well-known "Mesmeric look" directly. Those eyes revealed little, but Marcus had learned to read them over the last few years. He knew at this very moment that the Archbishop was on the edge of an eruption of Pontifical emotion, aimed directly at him.

Giovanni looked at the other man, who was transfixed on the pattern of the oriental carpet, appearing to count the threads in the weave pattern. "Do you have anything to add to this conversation?" Giovanni retreated from the brink of uncontrollable anger, a place he did not like to be, and redirected the conversation to the younger man.

"I have placed traps on the Internet as well as put out a query on several bulletin boards where I know he gets information. As of an hour ago, there was nothing. He has not surfaced in cyberspace as of yet. Once he does, I can get a fix on where he is working and will provide that information instantly to you." He never looked up nor changed the inflexion of his voice.

Giovanni marveled at the inner landscape that must be present in this man. Everything reduced down to binary code and keystrokes. The man had no feeling for humans; they were simply units at the end of the connection, nothing more. It concerned him, how this man had ever made it through the seminary. Someone else must have seen these qualities and yet here he was, ordained and in the Order.

Marcus was watching the eyes of the Archbishop and could only guess at the processing going on in that three-pound universe behind them. He did not know the extent of the current problem, but he had made a heuristic approximation about it and now it was time to test his theory.

"It has only been a week, Your Eminence. You know how he is, sometimes moody, reserved. He could be in retreat. . ." The words attenuated to near silence.

"In retreat? Retreat. . ." A ham sized fist smashed down onto the top of the file. "He killed the contact, picked up the package and disappeared. He has not made contact with anyone in Paris, Rome or Lisbon. He has something that is very important to this Office and you think he is sitting in a remote monastery praying to our lady for guidance." Giovanni could feel the blood surging through his head. At this moment one could say that he would take great delight in killing someone, anyone, with his bare hands.

"I only thought that. . ." Marcus had found out that his assumption was correct, that this was something considerable. For Giovanni to lose control this early in their meeting amounted to a declaration that the whole structure of the OSC was in peril or at least Giovanni's control of it.

"Thought what? You have worked in this office for ten years. You of all people know what we have done to protect this church and its flock." He wrapped his words in the self-denial of the Catholic religion. "Now, when it is of the greatest of importance, suddenly, one of your assets goes missing and we are supposed to put everything on hold until he finishes Vespers and walks in the front door of the Sistine Chapel, bundle under his arm and a new view of the goodness of humanity." Giovanni reduced his tone and amplitude of his speech to more befit his office.

"He has killed one of our only contacts too. . ." He straightened himself without finishing the sentence. He looked at the file again. "The Paris police are investigating a shooting of a meaningless member of society, who had a dead prostitute in his room. Granted, they are not looking really hard because they think it is all just another drug-related case. But we know, the three of us in this room, who the dead man is, what he represented, and who killed him. However, we are not going to tell the Paris police especially since the wild-eyed gunman happens to work for this office and now we don't know where he is. Would this look good on the cover of the 'Paris Match' tomorrow morning? 'Church involved in the dark underworld of drugs'. His Holiness might not think that anybody down here was doing their job effectively; and we would all find ourselves preaching masses in some place that does not have running water, telephones, or mail delivery.

How would that go down with that little demimondaine that you seem to enjoy screwing so much?"

"Archbishop, what are you suggesting. . .?" Marcus looked out of the corner of his eyes at the younger man, hoping that he would miss the reference. That was not very likely. Giovanni waved his hand to indicate the inappropriateness of the comment.

Giovanni sat back down and covered his face with his hands. "Fathers, we have but one role in our lives. That is to protect this church, its members, and those special friends that make sure we enjoy the privilege of serving. That is a heavy burden, but one that must be carried. The forces that oppose the church are many in number and growing every day. I do not want to see anything that looks like a holy war in my lifetime. So that is why it is imperative that you find him. Today! I don't care what you have to do, or who you have to bribe, lie to, or even kill. But find him." Giovanni turned his gaze back toward both of them. His words were like a sledge-hammer hitting an anvil.

Without a word or another look, the two priests left the office. The great doors opened and closed without a sound. Giovanni sat there looking at the window from the fourth floor that overlooked St. Peter's Square. The day outside was overcast and someone had told him he should take his cloak since it was supposed to rain. He looked at the Rolex on his arm and noted that he had forty-five minutes before his meeting with the Pope for the daily briefing. He spoke to the ancient dark furniture in the room, "Where are you and do you have my package?"

CHAPTER THREE

"We answered his prayer and relieved his affliction"
Book of the Prophets

The pre-Revolution shop on quiet rue St. Clair was nothing special, just a large shop window facing the pedestrians on a cobblestone street. The door was heavy and dark. Since before the First World War the business had been an antique shop. The windows had a film on both sides, a mixture of time, dust and smoke, the accumulation of lives that had passed in and out of the shop. The cave-like interior was filled with old, cheap trinkets, out of print books, photos and the residue of many people's lives, now long over and forgotten. But the shop was not visited by those that hunted for rare finds amid the dust of the ages; the clientele was limited to those that sought the services of the man that ran the shop.

The small Indian brass bell that hung on the door would announce their arrival, filling the semi-dark room with its tinkling sound. The owner would come out and exchange a few words to determine if they were qualified customers, or if they were just curious visitors to his world.

If he knew them, or found that they were seeking his services, he would lead them back into the labyrinth of smaller rooms that occupied the first floor. His was a trade not spoken of much in Europe today, but one nonetheless in high demand by a select few. He was a master gunsmith, unlicensed and living on the edge of society. Among his clients were many members of the country's security force, officers of the elite French military, and many notable citizens. They came with special needs, and he would always try to assist them, for a price. In truth, his business was marginally legal, for the proprietor preferred not to keep records. It seemed safer that way for all concerned.

Jean Philippe Emanuel Baptiste was a fourteenth century man in a modern world. He had grown up in the shadow of Notre Dame. His mother was a devoted Catholic who spent her days in church praying for everything: for more work for her husband, for her child's future, for the Germans to be driven out of Paris and for the war to end. She spent half her life on her knees in prayer. Jean's father was an instrument maker, woodwinds mostly. His shop was small and filled with the litter of a craftsman. He would spend more hours than was necessary putting endless coats of finish on an instrument he had rebuilt, until it reached a shimmering newness. It was here that Jean learned the skills of designing and building things of beauty.

His father was a quiet, bookish man who spent much time showing Jean how to hold a tool or how to work the metal until the fit was perfect. He would let Jean wander around the shop and read whatever book he fancied at the moment. Jean's mother and father both believed that Jean would go to Ecole St. Martin and become a priest. There was never a question of that. Jean did well in school, passing all of his exams with excellent marks. In the mid sixties he was accepted to St. Martin.

It was at St. Martin that the philosophical questions of life started their strange transformation of Jean. He read the great philosophers and his inquiries began. He found works on eastern religions that incurred the disfavor of the traditionalist fathers that ran the school. Their mission was to turn out priests who did not question the authority of the church. These men were not destined for great things. They were not the Jesuits deemed worthy to run the Church of Peter, but rather the laborers in the field. They were parish priests, who would hear the confessions of sinners, real and imagined, pray with the sick, bury the dead, marry the young, and preach a Sunday sermon that did not inflame or incite anyone to any action. They were the basic soldiers of the church.

But the years of Jean's education were troubled by increasing doubts and unanswered questions. He read about experiments of others with mind-expanding chemicals, the rejections of traditional values, the counter-cultures coming into vogue, and the rationalism that was replacing religion. By his last term, his soul was in agony. He had rejected most of his early beliefs and abandoned all of his desires for a future with the church. Jean knew discipline and loyalty. There was only one other place where he discerned those values had merit — he joined the elite unit of the Second Paratroopers' of the French Foreign Legion stationed on Corsica.

This was not the old Legion. It was no longer filled with the flotsam and jetsam of the world. It still had the traditions that made it the Legion, but the French were designing a new army, and the Legion's role was that of Special Forces. After Indo-China and Algeria, the Legion's commanders knew it had to change — to update — and so change it did. The Legion became a pattern for every army in the world to follow when designing a Special Force's unit. The men were not the drunken rabble that filled the Legion's ranks for two hundred years, but smart, tough young men. They were willing to give up five years of their lives to get the hardest and best training in Europe in one of man's oldest professions.

Jean found that his quiet ways and skills fit in well. He never complained, always followed orders, and built his body and mind into a machine, which could and would perform for him as he desired. His skills in metal and wood were soon put to a different use. "J. P.," as his colleagues called him, became the division armorer. He advanced well, making sergeant before his twenty-seventh birthday.

When Jean's enlistment period was up, he was offered a lieutenant's commission to reenlist. He decided to stay on with the Legion for another five years, doing what he had come to love, building and refining weapons. Sometime in the late 1970's he was badly wounded in Africa. He was given a small pension, the thanks of the Legion, and a Legion of Merit medal for heroism. Taking the money he had meticulously saved for ten years, he returned to Paris and bought the small shop cluttered with antiques, and occupied the living quarters above it. He moved his invalid mother into one of the rooms and spent his days refurbishing the lower rooms for his lodging, office and workshop.

Jean Philippe slowly built a business based on word of mouth and quality of the product. Old comrades would find him and ask for a favor such as filing down a sear, redoing threads on a barrel, or possibly even the addition of a silencer. Jean never asked questions; he would nod and say, "yes, that can be done." Money was not terribly important because he was comfortable. Jean had his savings, his inheritance from his father and his pension; he could live out the rest of his life in peace. Therefore, the shop profits simply augmented his already sizeable savings.

Jean's loves were his work, his books, his music and caring for his mother. If he went out, it was to the local bar to have a cognac with cheese and bread. He would sit quietly in a corner and read Hume or Kant. He would occasionally talk to locals if he knew them. Jean was happy with his life, doing the one thing that he felt he was really good at. . . . producing weapons without equal!

The small bell on the door rang out to signal that someone had entered Jean's domain. He pushed aside the heavy green curtain that separated his wood paneled office from the shop and stepped out. His leather apron, with scribes, ruler and pencils in the pocket, fit loosely over his thin and hard body, and gave him the look of a tradesman. A two-day old beard obscured the small white scars that littered his chin and neck. He kept his hair cut short for the ease of maintenance and, in his way, as a sign of respect to the Knights Templars that he had so admired since childhood.

The soft sound of Debussy filled the air of the small shop, almost like background music, below the surface, not loud enough to dominate, but just enough to fill the silent periods between thoughts.

The customer picked up a porcelain Madonna sitting between an open seashell ashtray and a cheap imitation of a Tiffany lamp. His hands seemed large in comparison to the small statue he held with a great degree of gentleness.

"Strange isn't it? That this is here among things which will never leave this shop."

"Not so strange, it is a relic of the past. It belongs here with all of the rest of the dead and forgotten things that people once cherished." Jean's voice was deep and soft. "How are you?"

Abdul walked over to him and took his hand. "I am out of time and on the run from everything." Jean motioned to the curtain.

Abdul entered Jean's comfortable living room. It was wood paneled and had a warmth to it, like an old sweater which one wears on cold winter afternoons. The two men sat across from one another.

"I heard from Mosey that you had, how. . . shall I say it, left your employer under less than desirable conditions." Jean produced a bottle of old brandy and poured two glasses. He handed one of them to Abdul and held the other.

"Mosey is still alive? That is incredible! Yes it is true, less than desirable. That is an understatement." Abdul drained his glass. "You know then about what happened last week?"

"He deserved to die, from what I read in the papers." Jean refilled the glass and handed the other man a cigarette.

"It had more to do with this than what was in the papers." Abdul pulled a small box from his coat pocket and laid it on the table next to Jean. It was a simple brown-wrapped package with no inscription, sealed with heavy tape. "That, my friend", he quietly stated, "could change the world as we know it. By the way, how is your mother?"

Jean pointed toward the ceiling. "Mother is old and tired, and misses my father. She lives in the past and thinks of me as a small boy. I care for her, try to get her to see old friends, but she only complains that they are too old to be around. She does not go to church anymore, not since father's death, but sits by the window and watches the people in the street. She too is a relic of the past like everything in this shop."

"Not you, old friend."

"On the contrary. . . me most of all! I no longer have a place in this world. My trade is a dying business, as governments feel increasing pressure to outlaw arms owned by citizens. When that happens, what I do will be a crime and someone will want to do something about that fact. Then what? Move to Brazil or some backwater in Asia? No, I don't think so." Jean stared into that indefinable, apparently hostile middle ground that such men see when considering their future prospects.

"It does not seem 'that' civilized out there to me. In fact, I still think that we are one step away from the caveman." Abdul pulled a notebook from his pocket and took out a small piece of paper. "Do you have one of these that you could sell me?"

"7.62mm? Small for you, nowhere near the stopping power of a Colt .45. Yes I have one, with or without serial numbers?"

"It does not matter"

"Let me get it for you." Jean walked into his workroom only to return a moment later unzipping a small black case. It held a Walther PPK. He laid the weapon next to Abdul, who picked it up and felt the weight.

"How much do I owe you?"

"Silly question."

"Money!" Abdul placed the gun back in the case.

"It is yours. You know that. What else do you need? You would not have come here just to buy a gun illegally. What can I do to help you?" Jean leaned back in his chair and inspected the man with the discernment and respect of a professional soldier.

"It is dangerous, what I would ask. It could cost you everything if any one found out. How is that for a hard sales pitch?" Abdul picked up the package and handed it to Jean. "Keep this for me."

SEAN DAVID MORTON - WAYNE E. HALEY

Jean looked at him. The silence became a living thing between the two men. He rose from his chair and walked into his workroom that was filled with lathes, mills, cases of parts and workbenches, motioning Abdul to follow him, Jean opened a trap door in the floor that revealed a safe hidden below. He opened it and placed the package inside, closing and locking the safe before replacing the floorboards that hid it.

"It would take an army to find the safe, in this room. If found it could not be opened without destroying everything inside. The safe is a Clifford, built in England. It does not have two rods inside the door but nine. The best safecracker in the world could not open it. The Clifford Company, twenty-nine years ago offered a million pounds sterling to anyone that could open one without a combination. The prize remains uncollected." Jean Philippe wiped his hands on a rag and leaned up against one of the workbenches.

"This is dangerous. Did you hear what I said?"

"Yes, so?"

"If I need that package, I will be in a hurry." Abdul placed the black gun case in his large overcoat pocket.

"Do you remember the date of our last meeting, in Africa, in Zaire?"

"Yes"

"Do you remember the exact date?"

Abdul thought for a moment. Then his eyed narrowed. "Yes. . ."

"If I am not here, you know where it is and how to open the safe." Jean turned back to the living room.

"Yes." Abdul returned to the small sofa and sat down. "Do you wish to know what you are holding for me?"

"No. I know that I have in my safe the life of the only friend I have still living. That is good enough for me. Should I expect visitors?"

"I wouldn't think so. Nobody knows that I come here, ever. And no one knows of the connection between us. Let us leave it that way." Abdul got up and headed to the front of the shop.

"No."

Abdul turned and looked at his friend.

"My back door leads to the alley. Going to the west will take you out on a busier street. You will blend in better there. This way." Jean showed the man out and watched him walk down the alley. In a low voice, not much more than a whisper, he called out "God be with you, my friend, for no one else will be."

Jean returned to his office and his open book, and listened to the last of the music drift through thoughts of other days.

***

Giovanni had a shrieking headache from his meeting with the Pope. He had gone over all the minute details that the Pontiff requested on the investigation into certain claims that the Church was holding funds that belonged to others. The Pope had ordered Giovanni and his staff to explore the possibility that this rumor had some merit to it. Giovanni had spent the last four hours eradicating the whole idea from his superior's mind. But the effort of dealing with the older man and his slow and simple style had driven Giovanni to the point of teeth-gritting frustration.

He had asked his secretary to get him a couple of aspirins and a glass of water, and to ask Father Marcus to come across the hall for a private meeting. Giovanni was standing at the window looking out into the gray sky and watching the pigeons plummet down on a dropped piece of bread on the street below. He saw the way they tore at the scrap and at each other in an effort to win the whole prize, not being satisfied with just a portion of it.

He smiled at this similarity between the pigeons and the average man.

Giovanni did not hear the door open and close behind him. He did not realize that he was not alone anymore, until Father Marcus quietly coughed. The Archbishop turned and then directed Marcus to the chair across the desk. "Please, be seated and make yourself comfortable."

"May I smoke?" Marcus still clung on to a habit that was losing favor in most of the world and especially in the rarified air of the Vatican.

"If you must. Please allow me to get you an ashtray, though. I do not want ashes on the carpet." He smiled and looked around, "the whole damn place might burn down and wouldn't that be a loss to the world?"

"Indeed it would. Thank you, your Eminence." Marcus pulled an artistically figured cigarette case from his cassock pocket and a flamboyant gold lighter. He lit his cigarette and blew a column of blue smoke toward the ceiling mural of the Archangel Gabrielle blowing his horn to call all the faithful back to the rewards of heaven. "How did it go over at the Palace?"

"As usual. A lot of "oh my" and "we must look into this" and the rambling of a senile old man that couldn't make a type one decision if he had too." The bitterness flowed out of Giovanni. He truly disliked the current Pope and was not about to hide it from the man he worked with on a daily basis.

"Oh, I see." Marcus stayed as neutral as he could. He was always concerned that one of these radical outbursts would happen at the wrong time and bring an end to his little corner of paradise that he wanted very much to hang on to.

"He was focused on the same thing again, 'what about the Jewish question?' He goes on about what happened sixty years ago and who is to blame. Did we do everything we could to aid them? Did we help the Germans after the war? Did we receive funds to keep on behalf of the Nazi's? Over and over again, until I am ready to scream. I keep telling him that there are no records of improper action on the Church's part, and that everything that could be done has been done. Thank God, today I was saved by some Cardinal having a crisis of conscience who needed to be seen immediately. I hope the Cardinal spends the next six hours spilling his guts out about every sin he ever committed or even thought about doing. Just as long as we make it to six tonight without him wanting to see me again, because, Marcus, his secretary told me that he is tied up completely for the next six weeks and he couldn't possible get me an appointment until after that time. In my estimation, that ranks right up there with turning water into wine as far a miracles go, I must tell you that." Giovanni smiled slyly and nodded to the other man. "Now, we need to do something about our little friend who has gone missing. Have we heard anything since I left?"

"Nothing at all." Marcus pulled his notebook out and thumbed through the pages. "We need to get some professionals out there looking for him. We have used the folks in the Nunciatures but they are starting to ask the wrong questions right now. These are not field agents, just clerks, and they are stumbling over themselves out there. If he is trying to hide, he will know by now that we are looking for him, and he is probably laughing at us at this very moment."

"Not for long, he won't be. We need to ask the questions in a more persuasive method, backed by a little muscle, I think." Giovanni looked at his watch, feeling that time was moving very slowly.

"You wish me to send out some of Gruppen Siben people?" Marcus asked the question with some disbelief. He knew that Giovanni would use them, but most of the time it was in some third world nation that did not require refinement to get the job done.

"No, oh Lord, no. Those guys are killers and arm breakers. No, we need a more subtle approach, I think. We need to borrow some of the folks from the Swiss Guards. Some of those people are pretty tough." Giovanni was jotting down a note on his folder.

"Father Leno will never let you use those guys. He is always belly aching that he doesn't have enough of them to protect the Vatican properly anyway."

"Screw Leno, that dumpy Sicilian bastard. Take this over to the Pope's secretary and have him obtain the Pope's signature on it." Giovanni handed Marcus the note he had been writing.

Marcus read it and smiled. "Of course, and this will start another little brush fire that will need putting out, won't it?"

"That is the idea. If they think over at the Palace that somebody is trying to attack the Pope again, they will give us all the resources we need to find our lost friend. So perfect — it all goes together like a Chinese puzzle box sometimes." Giovanni looked again at his Rolex. "If you go now, the Pontiff will still be busy with the Cardinal so his secretary can just go in and get the signature without much explanation. Then Leno won't be able to do anything but pass over the teams that we need. He may not like it, but he won't say a word in the face of the old man's endorsement."

Marcus nodded and left without another word. Giovanni walked back to the window and looked down into the street again. All trace of the bread was gone and the pigeons were sitting on the sills of the buildings again, looking content with themselves.

"Now we will find you." Giovanni noticed the message light blinking on his phone and decided to ignore it for a while. He interlocked his hands behind his back and continued to stare out the window.

CHAPTER FOUR

"For men are ever more taken with the things of the present than with those of the past"
The Prince - Niccolo Machiavelli

André Demmont had been a Swiss Guard for seven years. He had reenlisted twice to gain this assignment. He had dreamed of it as a boy, nurtured it as a man and accomplished it by the time he was twenty-nine. He held the rank of Captain in the most public protective organization in the world. Yet, as every soldier knows, Swiss Guards are nothing more than mercenaries. Since the Papal Edict of 1500, the Swiss were forbidden from finding employment as paid soldiers, with the exception of the small, elite group of men that protected the City State of the Vatican. The tourists and the faithful would come to see them in their ancient uniforms, standing by various doorways, clutching their great pikes and staring straight ahead. Few if any of the million or so visitors that pass through the Vatican in a given year, understand that there is a darker side to these costumed figures, who look as if they stepped from another era. The charge of security and protective service is just that, to protect and secure their stations just as rigidly as any other security force in the world today. For every Guard parading around in his yellow and black uniform, there are two in civilian suits, with 9mm automatic pistols in shoulder holsters, loaded and ready to shoot if the need arises. André had wanted this and now he was part of it. Now he too was in civilian clothes, walking the streets of Paris.

André was looking for a man; all he had to go on was two photographs and a small dossier on the man's activities in Paris. He knew that the order had come from up high in the administration of the Vatican, and that meant that they wanted this man found. The orders had been clear — find him, period. There was no room for failure — it was that simple. Go, find him and bring him back. Then his superior had said something that André had never heard in his career. "Kill anyone that tries to stop you, once you have him in custody. And if for any reason, you believe that you are going to lose him to another agency, the last resort was to kill the target himself." This told André that the target was so important that the Vatican would put up with a ton of bullshit and bad foreign publicity to acquire him. That awareness put shivers up and down his spine.

André's partner Teo, was a young sergeant from Lucerne who had been with the Guards for five years. A quiet, bookish man, Teo did his job and had little to say. André could tell that he too enjoyed his assignment at the Vatican, but he was not sure if this mission suited him. Teo was however the best shot in the Guard with a handgun and this gave André a feeling of comfort. He knew that if things got dicey, this man would provide whatever support fire was needed. Teo had not said anything about the job. He accepted the task, accepted his partner and accepted what was needed, with one slight nod of his head. On the train from Italy to Paris, he had said no more than a half a dozen words to André. He sat in the carriage reading a book on gardening and making notes in the margin with a pencil. When they reached Paris, he had placed the book back in his satchel, tossed it in the hotel room and became Andre's shadow on the back streets of the east bank.

André and Teo had been working their way through the list of known acquaintances of Abdul Hassan for two days. The people they interviewed said only that they knew Abdul casually and had no idea where he was or even where he lived. On the second day, they had found the apartment that Abdul called home. It was a spartan ten by twelve room, outfitted with a bed, neatly made; a dresser with two or three changes of clothing in the drawers; a desk with two works by Kahlil Gibran, the Arab author of *The Prophet*, which Teo had picked up and thumbed through; a writing pad; two pencils and one old fashion pen and ink set. The one picture on the wall was an old lithograph of Sir Richard Francis Burton, the British explorer and writer.

"Not much of a place to call home." André looked through everything again, under drawers and behind dressers.

"Hmm." Teo sat on the bed and looked out the window into the streets of Paris.

"More like a hermit's cave."

"Or a monk's retreat." Teo pointed to the building at the end of the street.

André walked to the window and saw what the other man had seen. "A mosque. Of course. He wanted to be near his own kind."

"Hmm. . ." Teo was writing in his notebook, listing all the shops that lined the street that Abdul lived on. He then compared his notes to the list that they got from the Vatican. He pointed to one name.

"A bistro frequented mostly by Arabs." André looked pleased. "Could this be of some service to us, you think?"

"If they will talk. Arabs are clannish by nature and normally not willing to talk about themselves to outsiders." Teo got up and went to the hallway. "But what else do we have to go on — two or three more names that will probably say nothing about him. It can't hurt."

As they walked toward the bistro, both men removed their ties and placed them in their jacket pockets. This was for two reasons — the first was to blend in with the denizens of the area, and the second was if they got into a fight, they did not want to give anyone an advantage.

Inside, the bistro was typical of small bars all over Europe. Pictures cluttered the walls and a zinc bar top that had been rubbed by the barman since the storming of the Bastille, crowned the dark wood. The room was dark and smoky, with small groups of men sitting around talking in their native tongues. The silence that settled on the room was deafening when the two strangers walked in and took the small table in the corner by the window. Orders were given and drinks arrived, two glasses of hot tea with lumps of sugar on the side. Both men sat quietly, waiting to be approached. It is common in many places around the world that new comers are sized up by the locals, when they have been foolish enough to cross into someone else's private reserve. It was no different here than it was in a Swiss bar.

It took about fifteen minutes when the first of the curious locals decided to see if these men were going to take root or depart from their world. He was a large man, with beefy hands that spoke of day labor and alley fights. He wandered over to the table and looked down with dull brown eyes that had seen too much hard living and drinking.

"Are you tourists that have gotten lost in the rabbit-warren lanes of Paris?" He surveyed each man for a response.

Teo took the challenge. "No, we are waiting for a friend of ours." He went back to his tea and continued watching down the street.

"You are not Arabs. How is it you could have a friend in this quarter?" He rolled his hands into fists and leaned them on the table heavily.

"No, we are not. But we have a friend who is and he told us to come here and wait." Teo turned away again, trying to irritate the other.

"Look at me, when I speak to you!" The large man raised his voice so that everyone in the bar could hear him. Teo knew that his actions would provoke a reaction. He had intended to get just this result. He looked up at the man, who hovered over him. He had noted that his French was heavily accented with the slurs and clicks of Arabic.

"Go away and leave us alone." Teo looked away again.

A well-placed kick from a heavy street shoe shattered the large man's instep as he reached to grab for Teo's shoulder. The man hit the ground, holding his foot and groaning. At this Teo got up and walked to the bar, where the barman was reaching for the old black telephone. Teo pulled it from his hand and ripped the cord out of the wall, throwing it across the room.

"I said we were waiting for a friend, Abdul Hassan."

The murmur ran across the room. The barman turned and looked at those at the bar. "I don't know him. Never heard of him!"

"Yes, you have, and I want to know where he is and whether you have seen him in the last few days?" Teo grabbed the man and pulled him across the bar. At this point the man on the floor started to get up, when suddenly he was catapulted across the floor, by a blow from André's foot. He stood there holding his H&K 9mm automatic pistol, aimed at the floor, where everyone in the bar could see it.

"Is this a blood feud?" An old man with white hair spoke.

"We are his friends and he needs our help. There are people looking for him. He is in a lot of trouble." Teo never took his eyes off the barman as he held him and spoke.

"So it is in all cities. We Arabs find no welcome here. This is not our land." The old man turned to gain the acknowledgment of the others in the bar.

"Where is he?"

"God knows. He could be anyplace. Abdul the Bandit comes and goes like the wind."

"Abdul the Bandit?"

"That is what he is called, by those who know him well. How do we know that you are his friends and not the assassins sent to find him?" The old man looked at the faces around him. "Describe him, if you know him. Would you agree he is a large fat man with a beard? That is the Abdul that we know."

"You know better — he is muscular of build, with a deep purple scar that runs from his mouth to the corner of his eye. Reads a lot and does not speak often." Teo had read the file and remembered it. André was more impressed than he could believe. Teo had gone far beyond what André would have thought to do, and he knew it.

"That is he. Only two people would know where he is, a girl named Jasmine in the flower shop around the corner, and Jean Philippe at the old antique store in the Latin Quarter on rue St. Clair." The old man walked over to the man on the floor and laid a comforting hand on him. "Now take what you have learned and leave us."

Teo released his grip on the barman and backed away holding his hands up as a sign of neutrality to the others in the bar. He pulled a roll of bills from his pocket and dropped them on the table. "For a doctor, to help your friend." He watched the way the old man commanded the room, with a gesture from his hand. He nodded and went out quickly followed by André who holstered his weapon as he left.

"I would have never believed. . ." André started.

"They are about other things. The old man was an Imman, a Holy Man, and he knew that things were about to get out of hand. He doesn't care about Abdul, only that the local police do not find out what they are up to." Teo lead the way quickly down the street and around the corner.

"How do you know that?"

"I listened to what they were saying."

"You speak Arabic?" André stopped and looked with amazement at the other.

"Italian, German, English, French and Arabic. I can read and write Latin and Greek also."

"That is not in your file." Andre' started to move again.

"And I hope it will not be. The flower shop is up here, I think."

CHAPTER FIVE

"The wise do sooner what the fools do later."
Baltasar Gracian

Jacob Isaac sat at his desk. The door was open to the garden. He had sat for an hour watching the birds that came to feed under the old orange tree in the center of the enclosed courtyard. As he finished reading the file for the sixth time that morning, he looked across his desk at two pictures in gold frames. One was the picture of himself, much younger, standing next to a gray battle tank, which he commanded during the Six Days War. Next to him stood Moshe Dayan, the one-eyed hero of Israel's glory days.

That had been the last time that Jacob had been in a uniform. Just after that photo was taken, he had exchanged his uniform for the civilian clothing of the Mossad, Israel's intelligence service. That seemed like such a long time ago. The straightforward life and death struggle of the soldier had been changed for the spy's world of half-truths and deception.

The second photo was of Ann, dear, sweet, complex, and wonderfully simple Ann. She looked so young in the photo. She had been so concerned about his new role as a spy-master, in a shadow world of light and darkness and had grown to resent the way Jacob kept her separated from his work and his world. The 70's and 80's were filled with hundreds of intrigues centering on Israel. During that period of time, he had not noticed the small changes in Ann. His days and nights had been consumed by activities and events that hopefully would never be printed on the front page of the Herald Tribune. It was far too late by the time finally Ann took him into her secret world and shared with him the horror that she had been living with for months. The cancer had so ravaged her body that she could no longer hide the reality. It took another year for her to die, most of it spent in hospital with Jacob constantly by her side. He knew the day he buried her that he interred a part of himself. His nights since then were filled with questions on his role in her death, and the eternal questions men ask of death — could he have done more or was this sad death preordained or predestined?

Jacob read through the file again. He looked at his watch and lit another cigarette. He knew that the meeting would start precisely at 1:30 and end precisely at 2:00. Thirty minutes was all the new ADI would allow to Jacob. The ADI, Assistant Director of Intelligence, was a man twenty-five years Jacob's junior, with no field experience whatsoever, an MBA who saw everything in terms of cost effectiveness and efficiency. Time and motion studies mixed with fiscal review. If he could not see the net result of an action in quantifiable terms of fiscal responsibility, he was against the action. If it were not for the power he had within the agency and the control he had over every life in the Mossad, he would have been nothing more than a joke at the water cooler. To most people, he seemed to be the DI, the Director of Intelligence already. He shadowed the DI everywhere. Gone were the days when an agent could walk down the hallway and poke his head into the DI's office and kick around an idea. Appointments were closely monitored and controlled. A pre-meeting brief was now required, outlining the nature of the operation, the necessary resources that would be requested, the financial implications for the agency, and the possible net result in both operational and financial terms. By the time someone finished one of these, the opportunity to take some positive action was usually past.

No one had seen the DI alone for over a year. The rumor was that the powers were grooming the ADI to replace the present DI within the next year and that he planned to change the whole complexion of the agency to conform to the rest of the government agencies, making it much more open to outside review and governmental overview. Jacob realized that if this came about, it was time for him to consider his long overdue retirement. He thought about the small beach cottage he owned in Haifa. He had always believed that he and Ann would spend their old age walking the shore and reading poetry to one another. It seemed now like it would be a lonely existence, surrounded only by memories and dark images of the past.

Jacob closed the file, got up, turned on the quiet window-mounted air conditioner and closed the door to the garden courtyard. He threw the contents of his ashtray into the garbage can and cleaned his desk off. This had become a tradition for him the past few months. The ADI hated cigarettes and the smell of them. He had put out a memo to that effect and recommended for health reasons that everyone that smoked should give it up. Jacob had laughed — for health reasons, he thought everyone should give up the intelligence business first. It was going to have a far greater effect on one's health than giving up smoking.

At exactly 1:30 the brief knock came on the closed door, which opened to reveal the presence of the DI and ADI as they walked in and sat down in the two waiting chairs. A few "icebreakers" were exchanged. Jacob noticed how gray the DI looked. He had seen the same facial coloration in Ann before she died. He felt bad for his old friend but as with many old friends, he could never bring himself to approach the other man on the subject of his health. It seemed too private a thing. As agents, they spent their days probing the depths of other men's psyches looking for weaknesses, and yet between old friends the discussion was never held. They had shared a world of secrets for more than twenty years and had known each other for ten years before that and yet he felt that any mention of a personal matter would cross a boundary that he was not entitled to cross.

Hiram, the DI was acutely aware of the strain that Samuel, the ADI was placing on the members of his staff. He would like to ease it, but time, tides, and the current of political realities had just made him tired enough not to take on this battle, one which he was aware would be impossible to win. He ruled the world of the past and Samuel belonged to the future. He feared for his friends, his department, and his country. He had been told that since the debacle in Norway, when Mossad agents killed the wrong Arab, things in his department would need to change, including the way the agency conducted business. The Knesset had decided that Samuel Goldstein was the answer. Hiram knew then it was the wrong answer, but these were different times. His thoughts were suddenly brought back to the immediate presence by the high nasal voice of the ADI.

"It would appear that you have spent a considerable amount of time this week on this project, Isaac, and without much to show for it." The ADI thumbed through the brief that Jacob had submitted.

"It could be a considerable problem." Jacob folded his hands on his stomach and waited.

"You see, that is one of the problems around here. Everyone is working on what 'could' be a problem and not what is." The ADI closed the brief. "We cannot afford the man hours or the financial expenditure to chase ghosts."

"I thought that is exactly what we did; chase ghosts, rumors, thoughts and dreams. Normally they lead us to someone who has a plan, and those plans often are not good for Israel." Jacob knew he was going too far, but yet he also knew that intelligence could not be reduced to a business school formula.

"No, it is not like that anymore. I want us to be a reliable organization that is fiscally responsible. I will not have my agency running after shadows, or spending budget monies that can better be used to upgrade electronic measures that have and do produce more and better results."

Jacob leaned forward on his desk and ignored the ADI completely. He looked at his old friend. "Does he speak for you, this agency, and the government? Was I out to lunch when they announced that you no longer run this department?"

"Now just a minute!" The ADI flushed with anger.

"No, I am still in charge. What have you learned?" Hiram looked at Jacob, also ignoring Goldstein.

"Let me point out that my appointment!" Hiram cut the ADI off in mid-sentence.

"Shut up!" The cold hostility was clear in his voice. He had nothing to lose anymore and knew it. He would probably be dead before this arrogant bastard could replace him.

"What do you know, what have you learned, and what do you believe?" Hiram pulled a cigarette from his pocket and lit it. Jacob pulled the ashtray from the drawer and sat it in front of the DI.

"Known — number one, that the Vatican has dispatched seven Swiss Guards, in plain clothes, to find one man, a courier, who has gone missing. The order came from the Archbishop of the Special Congregation. Number two, that they are running through Europe like a plague. The courier happened to go missing after the Post Office in Paris was closed. We learned this from someone working inside Central Police Headquarters in Paris." Jacob opened his file again.

"Post Offices don't close!" The ADI was glaring from behind his quarter-inch thick glasses.

"If you cannot maintain your silence, leave us!" Hiram never looked at him.

As an insider Jacob turned to the ADI, "A post office is a message drop on a courier route. The Postmaster in this case was a particular nasty little bastard who might have been killed by anyone. But there is more!" He scanned his notes.

"Learned — that the Vatican's agents have pulled out all the stops on this one. It is a covert operation on paper, but they are leaving a path of "scorched earth" behind them. They are talking to anyone who knew the courier."

"Okay." Hiram crushed out his cigarette and looked at his watch.

"Believe — something really important came down the pike. The courier decided to go in business for himself. He is probably going to try to cut a secondary deal with the black-robed bastards in Rome. Some of them don't like the idea of people mucking about in their private business. He has gone underground and it is important enough to send in shock troops with kill orders. We know that at least five other intelligence agencies are already aware of the operation: the Brits, French, Spaniards, Italians and the Americans. But for the most part none of them will know why it is so important, so they will only give it a quick consideration, since nothing is showing up on the Web or in electronic messages. This is totally a human intelligence operation." Jacob stopped.

"As should we." The ADI spoke through clenched teeth.

The DI held up one finger to indicate the mandate of silence had not been lifted, to the continued exasperation of the ADI.

"Why is it so important to us, Jacob? Catholic hit teams and a Catholic courier, I don't get it." Hiram sat back. They had shared too many years for him not to know that Isaac would have a good reason for all of this.

"The Post Office was the private property of Abraham of Warsaw." The words hung in the air. Hiram's face contorted into a mask of silent rage, his cheeks flushed with a flow of blood that no one had seen in months. His jaw set like a vice and his eyes were ablaze with a mixture of hatred and anger.

The DI let out his tension with a sigh and sat back. He looked at the ceiling and then stood. Walking to the doors to the garden he opened them. He turned off the air conditioner and walked out into the garden. He picked an orange from Jacob's tree. Sitting down on the low cement bench he started to peel it. Jacob knew this mood only too well. In twenty years he had seen quite a number of oranges picked from that tree. He looked at his old friend; he knew the body was failing but not the mind.

His contemplation was broken by the ADI standing to collect his papers. He looked at his watch again and was ready to deliver his latest diatribe to the DI concerning moving on to the next meeting.

"Sit down, Samuel! Listen, observe, and learn what this business is really about!" Hiram walked back into the room.

"I know what this business is about." His face had turned red, flushed again with anger. To be addressed in such a way before a subordinate was intolerable.

"No, you don't. Oh, you are smart and clever. You will probably be a good politician, but this is not about politics, the way you learned it." Hiram sat down and pulled his pen from the pocket of his white shirt. "Give me a piece of official stationary, Jacob."

Jacob complied and pushed it across the desk. Hiram began to write. At the bottom he signed the page and pushed the paper in front of the ADI. "Now it is the time for you to find out if you can handle this job."

The ADI read the letter. "I won't sign this!"

"For you to eventually take over this department and my office, you are going to need one final thing. That is for me to tell those people over in the Knesset that you can do the job. If you don't sign this, you will be looking for work by the end of the week." He turned to face the younger man squarely. "I still have more friends than enemies; I know where the bodies are buried that enable me to make that a promise." There was a stubborn hardness in Hiram's eyes that conveyed much more information than his speech.

The ADI signed the letter and handed it to Jacob. The latter did not read it, for he knew what it contained.

"Find out everything you can about the courier. Find out where he is and what he has taken. Get him, get to him first, Jacob; bring him here. If that does not happen, don't bother coming back yourself." Hiram stood up. "By the way, do you know the courier's name?"

"His name is Abdul Hassan, but for some reason, people call him Abdul the Bandit."

Hiram laughed a mirthless laugh. "Fits, Get him!"

When the room was empty again, Jacob picked up the letter and read it aloud.

"To whom it may concern: Jacob Isaac is working on a highly sensitive assignment for me personally. He is to be given all assistance possible and no request made by him can be declined. He has the full power of this agency and the government behind him. Ask no questions, only comply. Anything less will be considered an act of treason against the State of Israel." It was signed by the DI and ADI.

Jacob also knew along with handing him a 'Letter of Marquise', Samuel had handed him an insurance policy. He knew that Jacob could do this job without this type of letter and had done so for years. But what would the politicians think if they saw that their favorite fair-haired ADI had just signed a document that if examined in the light of day would mean the ADI's career, as well as his proverbial head on a plate.

"Hiram, you old bastard!" Jacob laughed. "You sly old desert bastard!" He slapped the desk with his hand and lit a cigarette. He picked up Ann's picture and looked at it. "Maybe sooner than we think, we will be walking on that beach, my love."

Jacob picked up the file and went out. It was time to find the real identity of Abdul Hassan, aka Abdul the Bandit.

CHAPTER SIX

"I realize that it is not my role to transform either the world or man."
Albert Camus

Mount Pontificate, built in the late 13th century, looms over the Back-trass Valley of northern Greece, located so as to escape the rampaging Muslim warriors. It had survived as a citadel of monastic belief until 1941 when the German Army had decided that it would make a perfect command center for the southern European front. Toward the end of World War II, the Germans had pulled out without destroying the monastery, unlike Monte Casino in Italy. After the war Mount Pontificate returned to its quiet contemplative work. The later part of the century saw several updates to the old facility — electricity, lights, running water, and a small hospital facility for the members of the community on the lonely mountain.

Through the cold, wet, and windy night, Abdul walked the final ten kilometers to the monastery. He had been fortunate early in the evening to get a ride in the back of an old sheep truck that dropped him off below the summit; that was four hours ago. He was tired, hungry and cold when he rang the bell hanging outside of the ten-foot high walls. He waited in the driving rain for an answer to his summons. Finally, one of the younger monks opened the small latched gate to the side of the main gate and inquired about the reason for his arrival. They did not receive uninvited visitors, and the hour was very late. Abdul pulled a waterproof case from inside of his coat and handed it to the young monk, who ducked back inside the slim protection of the wall to examine the contents. His eyes widen as he read the letter of introduction. He stepped aside and asked Abdul to enter, closing the gate behind them.

The interior of the monastery was silent. Abdul was shown to a private study with a fire still burning on the hearth. The young man stoked it and added a log to increase the warmth in the room. He bowed and made his exit.

Abdul removed his reefer jacket and hung it on the back of a chair near the fire to dry. He pulled another chair up to the fire and sat down, stretching himself out to relieve his cramped and cold muscles. Within a few moments the door opened silently and an elderly monk of impressive girth entered, holding the packet of documents that Abdul had presented.

The older monk, the Abbot of the monastery, sat down behind a large dark wooden desk in the center of the room. He lit an old brass oil lamp and turned up the wick. He took the documents and read each carefully; then laid them aside one by one. He sighed and placed all of them back in the leather case.

"This monastery has been here for nine centuries. The inhabitants have survived invaders, plagues, wars and the worst things one man can do to another. We have held to our simple contemplative beginnings, and somehow though all of that, we have been able to keep the world outside these walls." He sat and looked at his hands.

Abdul was now walking around the room, touching the heavy leather bound books that lined the office. "If only each of us had the time to read, understand, and apply the truths that each of these volumes contains." He moved his chair so that he would be in front of the Abbot and sat down again. "The world is still outside these walls and will stay there, if I have anything to say about it."

"But these!" The Abbot picked up the pouch of documents and handed them back to Abdul.

"These are only about giving rest, comforts and providing those services requested. I am not here to interfere with your solitude, your eminence." Abdul picked up the documents. "I believe you have added some new conveniences in the last two years."

"Yes, true. We did not consider them useful, but our Bishop ordered it and now we have a room that is nothing more than a curiosity to the other monks." He motioned to Abdul, "Is it here for you?"

"Me or someone like me. Could you take me there and provide me with a small amount of food and water?" Abdul stood and retrieved his jacket.

"At once. Vespers are at 4:00, but I feel that you shall not be joining us?"

"No, your eminence, with your permission I will occupy myself in other ways in your new room."

"As you wish. I shall have Brother Herbert attend to your needs. He will come by every few hours and see if you need anything. I think it is best if only he and I make contact with you, so as not to upset the other monks." The man was working at being polite.

"Thank you, Father. I will try not to disturb anyone and shall be out of here as soon as possible. But right now, I need some rest."

"Of course, at once."

The storm grew in its intensity outside the walls. There was little overt notice paid to the visitor walking down the hallway behind one of the brothers, only raised eyebrows when the stranger entered the cell that contained the "new things", as the monks called them.

CHAPTER SEVEN

"I knew I was being watched, but still I continued down the Street of the Potters.
If I stopped, I knew that which followed me would catch me or it might be ahead of me, already."
Diaries of Tatmas of Syria

The only light still shining at the Mossad headquarters burned in Jacob's office. He had just finished his third pack of cigarettes and his mouth tasted of nicotine and bile. The old agent looked at his watch and realized he had whiled away twelve hours of putting facts and dates together. His first step had been to send out a priority alert across Europe. Every agent available was to find out as much as possible in the fastest time frame possible and send it via embassy data links directly to him. He remembered what this business was like before the advent of computers and the safety of the public domain and one-way Zimmerman encryption keys, when special couriers had to move items by hand and sit in airline terminals for hours waiting for connections. Today, mere minutes after agents filed their field reports, these same reports were sitting on his desk, decoded and awaiting his review. The problem was now one of sorting through this mass of information to find the reality within it. Jacob knew his business too well. Everyone out there was going to file some kind of report, but only a few of them would contain some value. Many of the messages contained old information, outdated leads and even spurious data someone created just to have sent in something. But yet through all the noise, a signal was appearing. Jacob had a handle on this most slippery of characters and he knew it.

But the mosaic that was coming together only increased his concerns. The information was leading him to draw a new hypothesis about what this man was doing.

It had been fifteen minutes since he had called Hiram at home. After a brief exchange of greetings, Hiram asked directly what he wanted at such a late hour. Could it wait until tomorrow? Silence filled the ten kilometers of electronic void that separated them. Then Hiram said he was on his way.

Jacob picked up the glass of orange juice that had sat on his desk for hours and walked out the garden doors into the night and drank it under the stars. They seemed bright to him tonight.

He could not remember the last time he had just sat and watched the night sky. A slight feeling of pessimism — and foreboding — passed through him. He did not know if time favored his people this time around, knowing only too well that his country was less prepared than it had been in years. Dependence on others had encouraged them to believe they were safe and secure. Jacob did not feel that confidence. Viewed as one of the "old guard", Jacob was one of the last of the warrior monks that had defended Israel during the dark days when she stood alone against the whole Arab world. But the new politicians had promised changes and with those changes came the "warranty" of peace. He could still not imagine United Nations troops protecting Israel's homeland. The promises that were made at Camp David by this new American President would soon be put to a test if all that he worked on today were true.

Walking back into his office, Jacob rearranged the documents on his desk in an orderly fashion for his report to Hiram, so that he would not sound like one of the zealots over at the Wailing Wall talking about the end of the world and the coming of the Messiah. He placed three stacks together. The rest of the documents he laid to one side. The information that they contained was either too old, or irrelevant to the matter at hand. The old agent looked at the seventy plus pages that now held the story of one man's life and possibly the future of Israel. Jacob knew that if he raised this alert and was wrong, nothing on earth, or in heaven, that would exonerate him. However, if he was right, all the years of struggle, hardship, death, and loss would stand as mere prelude to what would be needed now. Every skill he had ever learned would be required for him to complete this task, and he knew that it would be his last action as an intelligence officer one way or another.

Jacob took his two pictures off his desk and placed them in the drawer. Opening his old battered copy of the Torah, he realized that he had not looked at a word of it since the night Ann died. He now quietly turned to a passage that she had once underlined for him and read it. Jacob did not think of himself as a good practicing Jew, but if there was one chance in a million for divine help, he prayed for it this night.

At twelve nineteen the door opened and Hiram Ben Latut, Director General of Israel's Intelligence service entered Jacob Isaac's office. This night, friendship was set aside and two professional spies sat across a desk, with the fate of their country spread out between them.

CHAPTER EIGHT

"Your wealth and your children are but a temptation."
Holy Koran

The flower shop was small and quaint, and a bit upscale for the neighborhood, but it had fulfilled a life-long dream for the woman who owned it. The people that lived near the shop would come by for wedding arrangements and funeral wreaths but little else, until the owner had hired Jasmine, a young Arab woman attending art school in Paris. Jasmine wanted to learn commercial design techniques to take back to the Emirates where she was raised. She privately believed that she would be able to make a better than average living working for one of the new start up businesses in Europe when she graduated, but her family expected her to return home. Jasmine knew that she would be required to abandon her western clothing, hairstyle, lipstick and perfumes, as well as the freedom of thought she had developed. It was taken for granted that she would return to the traditional culture of the other women in her society. That thought was repugnant to her. She loved the freedom that Paris offered her. Going without a veil and speaking to anyone that she wanted to had become a luxury that she would not willingly relinquish. It was so much different from the claustrophobic world that she had grown up in, where women did not think of going out and never talked to anyone.

By her mere presence and friendly manner, Jasmine had drawn many of the locals to buy at the flower shop, and she had met and befriended many different people. The arrangement worked well for her and for the shop's owner. Jasmine loved to be in the shop where the colors and fragrances delighted her senses. She worked as much as she could to afford all the little things that her family allowance would not permit. Her father, who had a prominent position with the government, paid her tuition and living expenses. So all the extra money that she made, unbeknownst to him, was hers to do with as she wished.

In the past few months she had been spending more and more time with a wonderful Arab scholar she had met. He was older than her, but that did not bother her. She perceived him as a walking library and travelogue. His name was Abdul Hassan and he was in Paris studying some of the old Arab text held in the special collection section of the Institute of Arab Studies at the University of Paris.

Jasmine had first met him in one of the thousand galleries near the Louvre. He was examining an old lithograph of an English explorer. When Jasmine commented on the remarkable eyes of the man in the picture, Abdul told her who the man was, Sir Richard Francis Burton and who besides being an Orientalist, had also learned the art of hypnosis while in India. Question upon question was asked and answered. Finally she had convinced him to have lunch with her. Joking with her, he had asked what her family would do if they saw her being so brazen toward a strange man.

"They would beat me until I was purple and blue on every part of my body." Jasmine had told him.

"Is this worth it?" Abdul had asked her.

"My body will heal, but to miss an opportunity to know someone like you would be a loss I could never recover from." She had looked at him with dancing and fiery eyes, seeking the secrets of his soul.

When they had finished lunch, he told her he had to go back to his studies. She refused to let him leave without a promise of another meeting and more conversations. Abdul had cautioned her of such inappropriate actions on her part, at which she just laughed.

It had taken her two weeks of harassing her Arab customers to find out where he lived and another week to convince the landlord of the apartment to open the door and let her sneak into his room and leave the lithograph which she had gone back and bought for him as a present. Four days later Abdul had walked into the flower shop one afternoon and stood there just looking at her face. She smiled and he did not. Jasmine thought she had greatly offended him. He had told her to lock the shop and get a coat. They spent the next four hours walking the banks of the River Seine. Abdul Hassan opened his mind and let twenty years of pent-up emotions rush out. All the bad and the good poured out of him. Jasmine listened, laughed and cried with him.

As they had sat on a bench near an ancient stone bridge, they looked at the contrast between them.

Abdul was six feet three inches tall, two hundred and twenty four pounds of rippling muscle, with a face lined and tanned from days and years in harsh weather. The scar that dominated his face ran from the corner of his mouth to his eye was a deep purple, but it did not take away from his handsomeness as much as enhanced it. He wore all black always, pants, turtleneck and coat. When he talked he moved his hands much as an orchestra leader directs a concert. Jasmine was small at five feet five, barely a hundred and ten pounds. Her short hair framed her olive complexion. Her eyes were the color of a raven's wing in sunlight. Her features were not beautiful as much as appealing. Jasmine had developed the habit of wearing bright lipsticks that contrasted with her dark skin. The mixture of dancing eyes and her round red lips moving quickly as she spoke her native tongue gave her whole face a radiance that Abdul had not seen in anyone in a long time. She preferred jeans to dresses and hiking boots to slippers but the way she wore them made the individual items take a life of their own. So there they sat, Abdul telling this twenty two year old girl the secrets of his soul. He had expected her to get up and walk away in revulsion. Instead she stayed and reached for his hand. At that moment, he knew when this current assignment was over there would be no more for him.

***

Jasmine had been reading a current Arab magazine when the two men in suits walked in, smiling.

"May I help you?" She closed her magazine and walked around the counter. She had only been introduced to the ways of gay men since she came to Paris, but she had learned to deal with this reality. It was not unusual at all to see a couple of men enter to buy flowers for their flat.

"You would not happen to be Jasmine, would you?" André was looking at some yellow carnations as he spoke.

"Why yes, I am. I don't believe I know you, do I?" She smiled becomingly.

"No, we have not been introduced properly, but I believe you are acquainted with a dear friend of mine." As André turned to look at the girl full on, his cold blue eyes took in all of her figure. "Abdul, Abdul Hassan."

Jasmine felt a cold shiver run throughout her body. She continued to smile, but suddenly knew that these men were of Abdul's other world. Not the world of the scholar but the one he wanted so desperately to get out of. They seemed much too worldly. She moved back toward the counter.

"No, I don't think I know anyone by that name; there are a lot of Arabs in this section of town; they have sort of claimed it for themselves; he may live here, but I am sure that I do not know him." She moved easily toward the telephone that sat below the counter.

"Enough!" Teo grabbed her wrist and twisted it cruelly. "We see that you know him and that you don't want to talk about him. Stop playing games, where is he, you little slut?" With his free hand, he backhanded her across the face.

"Sergeant!" André moved forward, but Teo turned toward him. "You have to realize that these people are animals, they only understand the direct method . . . Damn this little piece of shit! She is going to tell us what she knows or I am going to beat the living crap out of her and then, I may just do her for good measures." Teo turned back to Jasmine. He had never let go of her wrist. "You would like that, wouldn't you? It would just be like being home with the family; the brothers first do a sheep or two to get ready and then do the little sister . . . not much different, I would imagine."

Andre' scanned the streets for passer-byes. He knew they had discussed this approach, but abruptly he became aware of the fact that Teo was enjoying scaring the hell out of this child.

"Tell us what you know, or else I will let him work you over." The words sounded feeble when uttered in a flower shop.

"She is going to tell us, or she is going to die screaming!" Teo hit her again, this time harder. She fell to her knees, crying. Her face was turning purple from the blows he had landed. "Stop that you little bitch, you're used to worse treatment than this. Now where is that bastard, or I swear I will tear you apart." Teo let go of her wrist and grabbed a handful of raven black hair. He started to drag her into the back room.

"I don't know him. I've never heard of him." She forced herself to her knees for leverage and with all of her might she drove a fist into the man's groin. He let out a shriek and fell backward into a flower arrangement. André moved quickly forward just as she picked up the telephone. He jerked his head to see Teo pulling his weapon from its holster.

"No!" André screamed. Teo's face was contorted with rage.

"She ruptured me, that little whore! I am going to kill her!" Teo was struggling to his feet.

"No, that is an order!" André turned to see the front door of the shop open and an older woman come in; she saw the two men, the jumble of flowers and other pieces on the floor, and saw Jasmine trying to get up and out through the back curtain behind the counter. The shot from the H&K 9mm automatic inside the closed environment of the shop sounded like an explosion inside André's head. The older woman, the shopkeeper, had turned and was running into the street yelling for assistance when Teo shot her in the back. She crumpled to the cobblestones and a pool of blackish-red blood started to form under her. People were coming out from shops and houses. The sound of a police whistle could be heard in the distance.

"We need to get out of here right now." André yelled.

"The girl." Teo could hardly stand. The pain showed in his face.

"Forget about her, we need to get out of here and get you to a doctor, quickly." André put a shoulder under the man and started to use the escape route that Jasmine had used when leaving the shop. It led to a small alley used by the delivery vans. The agents made their way to one of the broader cross streets and found a vacant cab. They disappeared into the rush of the Paris traffic.

CHAPTER NINE

"Don't give in to every common impulse."
Baltasar Gracian

Abdul had been asleep for six hours. When he awoke, he did not know where he was. Lying on the bed looking at the stone ceiling for a few moments, he thought it was a prison cell or a crypt, but he could not remember how he got there at first. After washing up and eating some of the food that the monk had left for him the night before, Abdul opened his pouch took out the slip of paper that contained seven coded entries. Sitting in the only chair in the room, a straight-backed piece of hardwood that he was sure dated from the Inquisition, he started up the computer on the desk in front of him and logged in with the special password and code identifiers.

Checking his e-mail, Abdul scanned his new messages, only two current entries. Reading them, he concluded that the actions that he had taken so far had started a cascade within the hallways of power at the Vatican. They would be after him by now, turning over every garbage can and piece of cardboard in all the alleys of Europe looking for him. They, the ones that he knowingly offended, would want to hang his body on a high hook to rot for this little episode. Some people were going to get hurt, he knew that, but that was the price of this kind of endeavor. It was time to start the next phase of his operation. First though, he needed to leave a record for someone to find, just in case he did not complete this task. He also wanted to leave some track for others to follow if he did not make it back to Paris. He estimated that by now everyone in the courier route from that old Jew in Warsaw to the intended recipient would know that he had taken the package and that he was on the run. Abdul conjectured that there would be anywhere from twelve to fifty men hunting him all over Europe. This assumption was not based on pride or arrogance, but rather on experience and a genuine fear on two different fronts. The first was the package and the meaning of them items it contained. Secondly was the 'who' he had acted against. That was the key to the whole game. It had taken him nearly two years of covert work to position himself close enough to pull this off right under their noses. Trust had been slow to come, but in the end he knew that he would have his chance. With a little help from some rather rancid characters in high places, Abdul was able to get his hands on the evidence that would prove his theory. Now staying alive long enough to present the case to the right people was all that mattered.

Abdul pounded the keyboard in hopes that the person on the other end would understand the cryptic message and know what to do. Without this contact, he could not see this affair to conclusion, but rather would probably end up bleeding to death in some back alley somewhere.

Looking inside himself Abdul realized it was not death that bothered him — he had seen enough of that for two lifetimes — but it was the way it would come. Abdul could not image what it would be like to die at the hands of some psychopathic torturer who was more interested in hearing him scream than in what he had to say.

Calculating that he had only seven to ten days to complete his chore before they discovered him, Abdul watched his computer screen. With the passing of each day, his options were greatly reduced. Abdul looked at his watch and waited. If he was right, somebody was running like hell to get his message to their superiors and waiting anxiously for an answer. Time was agonizingly slow in the enclosed atmosphere of the monastery. He could feel his own heartbeat in his throat. What if those who had originally wanted the package now said no to his demands? He would have done all of this work for the past two years for nothing, and he would still end up dead. The people he was after were not going to let him walk away from this little nightmare. There would be too many questions for someone to answer. Secrets are only secrets if only a people know about them and it was clear that he was not supposed to be one of the inner-circle of those who knew. The people that hired him to do this job had to kill him, or they would be next in the chair answering questions.

The screen flashed:

"Yes . . . we want the package, it is ours anyway, but will agree to terms."

Abdul typed back quickly. This was the moment when this enterprise would all come together, or not, if they agreed to his two crucial conditions. He pounded them into the keyboard and sat for a moment rereading his entry. Then he hit the enter key. Hexadecimal code hit the telephone exchange in at least ten major cities. Monitor stations on the ground and in the sky would register the message but if they were not looking for it, it would not mean anything. But if somebody was online who knew what was going on, then this was going to be like the sounding of trumpets.

The screen flashed again.

"No. . . will agree to fee. . . but must bring it here."

He pushed the keys again.

"Neutral ground. . . Berlin, London, or Istanbul, no other choices. . . or else, it goes to Israel."

Abdul did not want to add the threat, but it was necessary if he was going to get these bastards to play the game. He also was well aware that this combination of capital cities would trigger Escalon, a dictionary-driven code breaking satellite system, developed by the Americans, to come online and alert them to potentially interesting activity in Europe. Most people were unaware that nearly every telephone, telex, fax and computer communication in the world was monitored by a half dozen governments employing thousands of people just to do this one thing. Billions of dollars, pounds, rubles, and yen have been spent to monitor what people think, talk about and do. Yet we still live day by day on the brink of worldwide destruction potentially initiated by an error in judgment.

Abdul looked again at his watch. He had perhaps six more minutes before someone could plug in enough equipment to trace back to this machine and find him. He waited.

"Istanbul. . . Wednesday, the old bazaar. . . three local."

Abdul clicked off the computer and sat back. He realized that the perspiration was pouring down his back and that every fiber of his body hurt. This was Sunday, so he had three days to get to Turkey and get ready. Those people, the ones who wanted the package would come, and they would come in force. There would be enough assassins in Istanbul to make the Old Man of the Mountain proud that he had introduced the term to the world during the Crusades. He thought about the old bazaar; it was an interesting location to make the exchange, right in the middle of the Arab city where most of this affair had started two years ago.

Picking up his coat, Abdul checked his .45 automatic and put his papers away. He walked along the long stone hallway carrying his valise, headed toward the front of the ancient building. He stopped and listened to the monks in the distant church chanting the words to an old liturgy, then continued toward the entrance of the ancient refuge. To himself he murmured, "Requiem in pacem."

The Latin invocation means, "Rest in peace."

CHAPTER TEN

"That I am I, that my soul is a dark forest."
D. H. Lawrence

Hiram sat down and lit a cigarette. He said nothing. Age and pain etched his face. He watched as Jacob opened the first of the three files, and with no formality, recited the facts in a monotone. This was two-dimensional knowledge in written format about a living and breathing human being. But yet it was an abstraction because it was about a stranger. Lines of data on a piece of paper were not the measure of man, they were only the blueprint. Hiram had always wanted more details than most intelligence chiefs about the men he hunted. It had to do with his desire to put flesh on bone and reason behind action. It was his way of being part of the human race and not turning into one of those people in the intelligence community that order a person's death without a second thought, who never really saw the target as a human being, with feelings, emotions, loves, hates and family. He hated this part of the job. He knew that when Jacob was finished, he and he alone would have to make a decision that would affect people's lives. He always hoped that he was right. He pointed with a quizzing look at the file that Jacob now held.

"A gift from a friend, just the thing we needed right now." Jacob opened the file and started to read from it.

"Raoul Dominic Lindquist: was born August 4, 1954 in Madrid, Spain. He was educated in England. His mother was English, his father Spanish. He was sent to the United States to attend Georgetown University where he earned a Bachelor's and Master's in Anthropology. Showing both special skills and understanding, he was soon after ordained into the Jesuit Order, and was sent to Rome where he completed his Doctorate in Philosophy at the Vatican University. Transferred to the Paris Diocese where he was teaching at the Ecole St. Martin. It was there he had an affair with a young coed. Order elders decided he needed some time to work out his views as a priest, and was sent to Africa, Zaire to be exact." Jacob paused only to turn the page on the report.

"Father Lindquist was running a mission station school and hospital in Zaire, when one of the many lousy little wars broke out and Africans were indiscriminately killing each other, along with any Europeans they could find." Jacob paused and looked up at his friend and boss. There was no emotion in his eyes. He was haloed in a circle of blue smoke from his cigarette.

"The French Legion was sent in to save a group of Europeans working in Zaire. They were a German operation, called. . ." Jacob scanned his notes. "Ortrag. It was a special weapons development facility where they were trying to replicate the American cruise missile guidance system and some chemical/biological weapons systems. They could not work on it inside Germany after the war, because of the treaties. But nobody told them they could not develop it in some backwater in Africa that nobody gave a damn about."

"The Legion passed through Lindquist's village on the way to their destination, the Ortrag facility. Lindquist convinced a young commanding officer to take his people along rather than let them be butchered by rebels. The French did this, but suddenly find themselves up against a bunch of "rebels," armed with AK-47s and RPGs — all from eastern block countries, all sympathetic to the poor natives being oppressed by God-knows-who this time. So what had been a tribal war between different local factions abruptly turns into a twentieth century conflict with automatic weapons and high explosives, with a bunch of Europeans in the middle of it. This tribal war had been going on between the Hutus and the Tutsis for thousands of years. But suddenly they got really effective at it when some fool handed them gun powder."

"Anyway, this group of rebels just happened to have six East German advisors, a ton of equipment, and no less than division strength. It seems like Moscow had decided it wanted both the strategic and tactical information that Ortrag had developed. Taking it under the guise of a local war was going to be easier than trying to steal it from the Americans. So they sent the rebel group with their advisors in to make it to the Ortrag facility in Katanga Province and grab the same information that the French were going in for. It seems like everyone suddenly wanted this information and here is Lindquist in the middle of this mess. It must have been one hell of a firefight. There were two days of running gun battles through central Africa and not a word got out to the press. Well, it seems like the good father was much more of a solider than a priest. He not only got most of his people out of the slugfest and all the wounded French Legionaries as well, and single handedly destroyed two companies of rebels with their advisors just for good measure. He topped it off by saving the young French officer who originally had aided him. The good father got pretty shot up in the skirmishes, three wounds to his body and fragment of a hand grenade ripped open the side of his face down to the bone." Jacob paused and handed Hiram a black and white photo of Father Lindquist showing the scarred face and penetrating eyes.

"The French wanted to give Father Lindquist the Croix de Guerre, but the Church officials were insanely opposed. He was sent to some monastery where he was buried up to his eyeballs, praying for his soul and scrubbing the bathroom floor with a toothbrush. A typical Jesuit response, I believe. Nobody considered the fact that the man saved the lives of one hell of a lot of people and aided in the French in keeping some mighty valuable secrets out of the hands of the folks at Moscow Center. But there is that whole 'thou shall not. . . stuff' that Jesuits deal with."

Hiram laughed dryly. "That is in our book also. In fact it started in ours. . . . but I suppose I can't expect you to know that, you sacrilegious bastard."

"I keep the Sabbath!"

"Only by drawing the blinds over the windows, watching television from Syria and drinking milk with your ham sandwich." Hiram looked at the picture of the young priest. "He must have been a nice looking chap once."

"Not anymore. That's one beauty of a scar on that fine young face. It gives him the sinister look that led to his nickname. Abdul the Bandit." Jacob paused.

"Yes, I wondered about that before, but now it is even more intriguing."

"It seems like the next time that Father Lindquist or Abdul, as we shall now call him, showed up was two years ago. He was working in Western Europe as a courier. Moving everything that one can imagine; documents, bonds, money and people. Abdul worked for some of the worst people in the world. He kept moving up, getting higher level of assignments. Hell, at one point, we had used him to move some questionable material to the Finns. We did not want any involvement with it, so some bright young chap in the Paris office employed Abdul for the purpose. When the report came back from Paris Central, you could have knocked me over with a feather. Abdul has been employed by at least six different agencies and nobody knows how many private actions in that two-year period. The man is always on the move. He only shows up in Paris to pay his rent and sees an Arab girl that is a student in one of the academies. No one knows if they are lovers or not. But. . ." the words hang.

"So we have a renegade priest turned provocateur and courier. Tell me about Abraham's involvement." Hiram got up and walked around the room. Jacob could tell he was also starting to piece things together.

"Abraham was contacted about 18 months ago by someone from Saddam's staff who wanted him to handle a special package. It seems they wanted to exchange a chemical/biological warfare agent, which was genetically keyed to a particular western power, for a free hand with some of their neighbors." Jacob looked up at Hiram.

"Let me guess which group the genetic specific material was keyed to. . ." The sarcasm was heavy in his voice.

"Yes, of course. . . us." Jacob looked at his file. "It would easily infect anyone with Eastern Mediterranean Syndrome or Tay-Sachs and scramble their immune system to the point they would be dead in less than ten months."

"Somebody built this little gem?"

"Probably the same lab that designed HIV or AIDs or whatever else they call it this year." Jacob refilled their orange juice glasses.

"Who the hell would buy that!?" Hiram pushed his hands through his silver gray hair.

The last words hung in the room for a few moments, and then suddenly Hiram turned and looked at him.

"You don't think. . . ?"

"Yes I do. It figures. Think about it. An ex-priest, defrocked and angry, infiltrates the smugglers route to get his hands on something to hurt those who hurt him. The church is attempting to expand its influence in the Middle East to try to abate the growth of Islam. That old Jew in Warsaw has been trying to kill all of us since he went over to the Nazi's in '41. He hates Israel and all it stands for. He was shunned and never allowed to immigrate, so he has helped every crazy bastard who has concocted a plan to destroy us since '48. You've got every available Swiss Guard the church has shooting his way across Europe trying to find our friend with the goods. We have seen similar patterns in the past, but not as overt as this. The belief is that some group out there that is still trying to finish the job they started so long ago. But as we get closer to our friend Abdul, we learn more of the truth. What do you think our options are on this, boss?" Jacob sat back and watched the other man.

"I hate it when you call me that. I know you already have a game plan, but you are going to make me think that it was my idea, like you always do. Not tonight though. Tell me, besides killing that old bastard in Warsaw, what else can we do?"

"If I could have killed Abraham, I would have done it twenty years ago. That is not something that we seem to be able to do. . . and besides, he is not the problem right now. It is the priest and the package. We need to find him, make a deal for the package and find out what it is that could do so much damage to our people. If we fail at that, we need to kill him and take the package.

"What about the Catholics?"

"I don't know yet. I can't figure out what they are doing. It has to be a covert operation being handled by a small faction inside the church, because if it has the blessings of the higher ups or if all of this is an attempt to begin another Crusade, then we are all in real trouble. I hope that will sort its self out. Right now, I think there is only one thing that needs doing and that is finding Abdul the Bandit."

"You. . ." Hiram pointed at him. "You find him yourself. Use whoever and whatever you need but I want you on the ground, personally conducting this operation."

Jacob was shocked. He had not believed he would ever hear this from the man who grounded him so long ago. "You told me that I would never go back out in the field."

"That has all changed. I don't want one of these ass-wipe kids around here trying to make his mark on something that could mean the end of our country, as we know it. No, there are no regulations. I don't care what you do, as long as you get him. Jacob, the lives of countless living and unborn Jews rest tonight in your hands. I know you are as tired of all this crap as I am, but once more, old friend, we must stand the line for our country. I cannot. You and I both know that. So it comes down to you." Hiram had tears in his eyes. He looked away. Jacob hesitated, then asked quietly, "How long?"

"Weeks at best . . . but that does not matter. Get him Jacob, do what ever is necessary again, my old war-horse, then come home and enjoy what you have earned."

"A lonely house by the sea." Jacob thought about Ann's picture.

"A house by the sea in a free country that is still ours."

CHAPTER ELEVEN

"Give warning to mankind, and proclaim good tidings to the faithful: their endeavors shall be rewarded by their Lord."
Holy Koran - Book of Jonah

The foggy morning had given way to a bright afternoon. The hillside outside Athens where Abdul sat reading his notes was warm. The air felt clean, after last night's rain. The sun was a brilliant orb in an azure sky. Abdul had decided to wait until night to make his way downtown to the place where he could schedule his flight to Turkey. He wanted to reduce the space of time where anyone could see him clearly. Beside the night offered its friendship to him. Knowing the night well and how to work with it gave him some degree of comfort. He had found a small café and bought some cheese and bread, which he consumed with a liter of clear water. This place seemed remote from the streets of Paris and the package. Noting the ruins that lined the hillside, he remembered that he once knew their names, when they were built and by whom, but that seemed a long lifetime time ago. It was almost if that man who he had been, the professor, was somehow a figment of his own imagination.

Abdul thought through his current options. He knew who would come to Istanbul, and what kind of force the OSC had at its disposal. The people that wanted the package would act swiftly. Abdul knew Giovanni would insure that the package was intact, and then he would muster everything they had to get rid of Abdul and any trace of his involvement. The OSC would want their money back, but if they could not get it, they would still eliminate Abdul. They could not rest knowing that he was still alive, enjoying life at their expense. It was that simple. Thinking of the meeting place, Abdul pondered the start of the old Ottoman Turk Empire, named for a small emirate peopled by the descendants of *Osman*, called by the Europeans the Ottomans. In 1331, ibn Battuta, the Arab Traveler, had noted that Ottomans were barely able to keep control of their lands. A century and half later, the Ottoman Turks were knocking at the doors of Europe through Greece, and having conquered all of North Africa, were contemplating the invasion of Spain. He mused that great things often start with small actions. What would this meeting bring to the world? It could result in the changes of governments or even a new world order, if he failed.

Abdul's cell phone buzzed at his waist. Only four people had this number, or at least he hoped that was still the case.

"Yes." He waited through the momentary delay caused by the satellite transmission.

"If I were to tell you that someone knows about you, would you be surprised?" The quiet tones of Jean Philippe filled the airwaves.

"I probably wouldn't be, but it would be interesting to know who they are." He knew that this call would only be made if it were truly important.

"Their identity is the issue. It appears they are looking very hard for you and taking huge chances. It would seem that they don't care who knows. They broke up the bistro, demanded to know about you, killed the old lady Garnier at the flower shop, and worked over Jasmine pretty well." The line was silent as Abdul looked off at the haze that hung over Athens.

"Is she alright?"

"She is bruised, hurt, and scared. But it sounds like she got the best of one of them." Jean Philippe could feel the heat and silent anger passing over the line.

"Where is she now?"

"Upstairs with mother. She followed your instructions and came here immediately after the incident."

"What if they come again there?"

"What if they do?"

"I need to know who they are and she does not need to be a part of it."

"She won't be. Tonight, in about an hour, I am taking her to the airport. She is going home for a little while. I thought that best."

"I think you're right, thank you."

"Don't mention it."

"I need to know who they are. If they come, can you find that out?"

"If they come."

"Midnight tonight. . . the shop phone."

"Oui."

The line went dead and Abdul closed the phone. Who would search that hard when he had already made contact? Time delays, information flow problems or just a double cross; all of these ideas ran through Abdul's mind. It was interesting the way they were trying to find him. He got up and headed down the road in the gathering evening gloom. It would take him a few hours to get to his destination.

CHAPTER TWELVE

"For nothing is fixed, forever and forever and forever. . ."
James Baldwin

It had taken Teo almost six hours to recover from the hit in the groin inflicted by the young Arab woman. He found out from the doctor at the clinic that he was only bruised. He would be sore and the swelling would probably be hard to move, but he would live, even though a few hours before, Teo was sure he was going to die.

André had checked in with his control in Rome, but it seemed as though there was some confusion as to what to do next. The Swiss Guard looked at his list and realized that he had only one more name to investigate before contacting the situation desk in Rome for further orders. The killing of the old woman at the flower shop bothered him greatly. André had determined years previously that he could take a life if it was in the line of service. What Teo had done seemed to be different. The other thing bothering him was Teo's explosive temper. He wanted to quickly finish this assignment and get back to Rome. He would continue to search, but he wanted a different partner and Rome was too distant for a replacement to be moved into place right now. Acknowledging this fact, he went down the hallway to the front of the clinic and found Teo sitting reading a magazine.

"How do you feel, Sergeant?"

"I am passable, but I would like to get my hands on that little bitch."

"Enough of that. We have one more contact to locate. If instinct tells me anything, he will have gone missing by the time we get to his shop." He looked down at the other man. It seemed oxymoronic to him, this almost shy young man, so quiet on the outside, while a typhoon raging inside. "Let's get a cab, if you're up to it."

"I am not doing anybody any good sitting here. So sure, let's go, but I tell you. . ."

"Teo. . . nothing, not a word." André held up a finger to indicate he wanted no mention of the girl again.

"Yes sir." Teo returned to silence. But by the look in Teo's eyes, André could sense that a plan was forming in his head.

***

Jacob had received another report from Paris, a shooting in the streets. Nothing unusual for a major metropolis, with the exception that it had occurred in the Arab section of Paris, and the suspects were two men that were not Arabs. Paris has always been a hub of activity in the intelligence business, and every agency in the world has dedicated resources and assets living and working there. When the first alert went out, most routine activities came to a stop and all eyes and ears started to find any lead that might assist in the current assignment. It had not taken long for someone to figure out that the shooting was not like most. Jacob looked at the computer printout and wondered if someone else was starting to play rough.

Jacob considered calling his counterpart in the American intelligence service, but then thought better of it. If they were unaware of these recent activities, it would not aid his cause to let them in on it. The British and the French were notorious for being unhelpful and even down right dangerous to bring into any enterprise concerning Israel. The other smaller countries had agencies, but most would not have the level of sophistication necessary to handle this type of operation without leaks occurring. Others were looking for this man, Abdul, but why center on Paris? He had alerted all his European and Mid-Eastern field stations. Yes, the man worked out of Paris, but that did not mean that he was there. Jacob looked carefully at the stack of reports. What if they don't understand what he is doing? He rubbed his chin and thought about who he was dealing with. Jacob believed he knew something about this Abdul. He was smart, well educated, dedicated and probably very dangerous, all the ingredients that Jacob would look for in a field agent. The problem was that he was a lone wolf. This made it harder to find people that truly knew anything about Abdul. The man had to have some kind of communications, safe houses and people that knew enough about him to be of assistance. Jacob realized that Abdul had gone underground and was moving quickly, but where to? That was one of the questions he put on his decision matrix for analyzing the problem at hand.

Abdul would have to make contact with someone, to sell the package. Who? It was clear that he was smart enough not to use a middleman, which is how he had got his hands on the material to begin with. Someone had trusted him. He would not make the same mistake. Who would buy it? There was a limited number of buyers. A half a dozen Arab countries and ten groups of terrorists, all funded by one or two of those same countries. No western power would touch it. It was too specific, targeting only Israel.

Then there was the Vatican, but somehow this still did not make sense. Jacob wrote down one word on his pad, "Vatican" with a question mark behind it. But yet, when he read the report again about the Swiss Guard storming through Europe, it all came back to the Catholics. Why? He added this to his list. Too many questions, not enough answers yet to make any kind of positive move. Jacob wondered if the ADI had been taken into any kind of confidence yet about this operation. If he had been, he would probably be rolling on the floor of his office holding his stomach and wanting something for the pain. The cost of this adventure was going to be huge. Jacob knew that he was going to have to buy information. That was always costly for what one got in return, but it seemed at this point the only way to find out the unknown parts of this puzzle.

Jacob called down to the situation room to check the status of the program that he had set up yesterday to handle what was being called the "Abdul Problem". He waited while someone picked up on the other end.

"Sir."

"Can we get our hands on the list of Swiss Guards, descriptions and possibly photos of them? The ones that were sent to Europe?" He made it a question, knowing that the person on the other end of the phone would understand it as an order.

"Let me see what I can do, sir."

"Fine." He replaced the handset and thought how strange it was that there had developed a whole different way of talking to one another in the intelligence business. But then few, if any, careers offered such a quick chance to die if discovered, making oblique language a life-saving skill.

He called the situation room again and told them he wanted field assets to cover every major airport. It would take two or three agents at each one, and it was a long shot; but he quipped, "Let's not sit on our hands" to the agent at the other end of the wire. There was only a "sir" in reply and then the line went dead. They would hate that order out in the field, boring work walking around an airport talking to everyone that you had made a friend of with in the last five years and asking each of them the same questions. Showing a picture of someone and not telling your situational friends anything about him, while you are sweet talking them to get what you want. But that is the nature of the business. Jacob had done it and so had every other agent in every service of the world. This kind of canvassing was the day-by-day grind that left many people hollow and empty to all human emotions. Playing the part of someone who cares and all the time, having the merest scraps of information to go on and never knowing the whole story behind what you are doing. Jacob slammed his fist down hard on his desk. The exasperation flowed out of him in a barrage of Yiddish profanity. "Where are you, Abdul, and what are you doing!?" He yelled at the four walls that were both his office and his cell.

***

The small, dark, hard-faced man sat at his desk in the dimly lit office in the basement of one of the auxiliary building behind the main complex of the Vatican. A perpetual frown covered his face. His olive complexion spoke of the southern climes of Italy where he was born and raised, Sicilian by birth and disposition. At the present moment that disposition was making itself known. Father Leno, head of the supervision section of the Swiss Guard, had been up all night rearranging schedules to cover all of the important activities around the Vatican for the next few days. He was responsible for the operations of this group of dedicated men. Having half of his staff pulled to go running off through Europe to hunt another assassin had caught him off guard. But a person does not ignore orders from his Holiness. Leno believed that if the Holy Father thought it wise to conduct this action, he would certainly not question it. Receiving the orders to send a contingency of Swiss Guards into Europe on a special assignment and not being made privy to the reason was something unusually to Leno in these times. His job had been to select the men. Someone else would contact them directly to brief them. Then Leno had to find the resources necessary to cover the regular work in Rome. He read the flimsy that was just delivered and then looked up at the priest who had brought it in.

"What does he mean, recall them immediately?" Father Leno's Sicilian heritage was surfacing and he had not learned to hide his deep inbred Latin temper in all the years he had been in the Vatican. He got up and fumed for a few minutes at the need for of all this cloak and dagger stuff. It did not suit him at all. Leno preferred well organized and clockwork precision in his duties. This was not the way things were done.

The younger Father stood looking at his shoes and studying the pattern of the carpet in the small but comfortable office. Finally, when he thought it was safe to offer-up a comment, he noted.

"Notice who signed it, Father?"

Leno studied the note for another minute. He then looked up expecting an explanation to this cryptic statement.

"Call him if you think that something else should be done." The young man was willing to brave the rage of the old priest rather than go back upstairs and try to play intermediary between these two warring factions.

"You must be crazy. Nobody is going to call him and ask for an explanation. You know that."

Leno sat back down at his desk.

"Then I would suggest that you follow his instructions and recall the Swiss Guard back to Rome and prepare them for another briefing." The younger man was showing deference in his actions, but not his words.

"You would, would you?"

"Yes, otherwise I am sure the Archbishop will find a nice small parish for you, somewhere in the darkest part of Asia. It would better suit a blowhard like you, than this comfortable suite in Rome. I think it wise on your part to follow orders and stop playing some kind of Prima Donna that needs a reason for every action." The younger priest brought his gaze up to meet the older man's. A recognition of authority by virtue of association flashed through Leno's mind.

"I am sure you are right. I will have them recalled at once. Each team of Guards must check in twice a day, so it will be a little later for some than others. I should be able to have them all here by tomorrow afternoon."

"There will be a briefing for them at 3:00 in the council chambers on the third floor. Make sure they are all there, Father Leno. That is crucial." The younger man turned and started to walk away.

"God bless you my son, you are a true servant." Father Leno looked down at the list that he had to call.

"Yes I am." With that Father Anthony returned to the rarified air of the upper level of the Vatican's political hierarchy.

***

Abdul entered the travel agency just before it closed at 7:00 p.m. The young woman looked at her watch, and trying to be polite, motioned for him to sit down next to her desk. Abdul apologized repeatedly for keeping her late, but then, it was his mother, taken ill in Turkey, and he needed to get her back as soon as possible. No, he did not want to get return tickets just yet. He was unsure how long he would have to stay. Abdul implied that he had never been out of Greece. Had she been to Turkey? If so, was it true what they said about Turkey? He kept up the chatter for the entire fifteen minutes it took her to confirm a seat on the morning flight to Istanbul and charge his credit card. She needed to see his passport. Oh, that was back at his house. The travel agent explained to him that he had to have it with him to clear customs going and coming.

Abdul talked about going to the north once to see a sheep show, but then he had traveled via bus. She smiled and finally handed him the ticket. Abdul left and she hurriedly locked the door and went down the street. He sat in the café across the street and had coffee and watched the passing throng of people for the next two hours.

At nine o'clock he walked back down the street and surveyed the neighborhood. It all seemed quiet. Abdul stopped in front of the travel agency and laid his valise against the center of the doorframe. Then he leaned against the valise. He took the small electronic detonator from his coat pocket and activated the red switch. The microcapsule of explosive that he had earlier pushed into the lock before he left made a muffled sound. The effect of the CN5X high explosive shattered the locking mechanism without causing any other damage to the door. The valise absorbed most of the shock wave and sound.

Abdul quietly slipped into the darkened interior of the travel agency and started up the computer. He pulled a slip of paper from under the blotter, which the girl had used to log onto the airline reservation terminal. Typing the necessary keys and entries, he modified several screens of data, then turned on the printer to produce the new ticket. This one would match his passport and no one would be the wiser, he hoped. He took a small plastic bottle from his case and poured some of the contents around the room. Opening the file cabinets, he made sure that he poured enough mixture on all the papers to aid in the fire, then set a small device on the floor and flooded the area around it with the liquid. He walked back out into the street and made his way around the corner and down toward a cabstand at the end of the block. As he got into a cab, he heard the first alarm bell ring. It would take a few minutes for the fire company to respond and by then the whole building would be burning. Abdul felt bad about the losses he would cause people and the time it would take them to recover, but then again, it might not matter after all. He directed the cabbie to take him to the airport as he had a late flight to catch.

CHAPTER THIRTEEN

"Is every person able to spin a thread from the sinews of his longings and affection and attach it between his soul and a departed soul?"
'IRAM: City of Lofty Pillars' Kahlil Gibran

Jean Philippe had learned as much as he could from Jasmine as he escorted her to the airport for the flight home. She was still reliving the incident and would for quite awhile. He knew that was how the human mind worked, and was briefly, but compassionately sorry for what she would experience. She would go over and over it. She would wonder if it might have gone differently, or if she would have been raped or murdered. The reality of seeing her friend killed in the streets would only increase the intrusive images that would haunt her during quiet and early hours of the morning, when it seems like the very corners of the room take on a life of their own. But she would heal. She was young and still had many things to look forward to. This he also knew.

He was working in his shop on an old, small automatic that someone wanted to give to his wife for protection. He had been asked to make it workable and safe. Dvorak's string serenade Opus 22 played in the background — it had just entered the Larghetto movement, four minutes and twenty nine seconds in length, if played correctly. He heard the small tinkling of the shop bell, and while it was late for most people, many of his customers did not come by during normal business hours because of the nature of their business. He wiped the gun oil from his hands and walked into the front of the shop. A large blond man in his early thirties stood looking around. The man turned and smiled, but only with his mouth. His eyes never changed expression.

"Yes, what can I do for you?" He noted a movement to his left in the shadows. Someone was standing next to a hutch that held his old books and glassware.

"I am looking for someone." The other man picked up a piece of porcelain and acted as if he had lost control and it hit the floor shattering into a hundred pieces. The move did not get the response André and Teo had expected. Jean Philippe did not move forward to inspect the damage.

"That will be a thousand francs." He watched with his peripheral vision the movement as the man in the shadows tried to move behind him.

"But it was an accident, sir, I promise you." André unbuttoned his jacket and raised his hands in supplication.

"So is this!" The Jagger-Panther throwing knife is known in the world of professional soldiers as the most perfectly balanced piece of steel created by man. It is eleven inches from tip to end and in the hands of an expert it can hit a target at thirty paces every time. The effect its upper serrated edge has on human flesh is a surgeon's nightmare; it rips and tears through muscle and bone like a high velocity round of ammunition. That was exactly the effect it had on Teo's windpipe. The knife left Jean Philippe's hand and in less than one second had driven itself through the man's throat and lodged in the hutch. Teo hung there for a few seconds, and then his own dead weight pulled him to the ground cutting a larger gash in the side of his face before the knife dislodged from the old wood.

André had swung around to see the action to his right and then reached for his weapon in the shoulder holster. He had only half turned back when he saw the barrel of a French made MAB 9mm pointed directly at him.

"There is this great old American film with Clint Eastwood. He says, 'do you feel lucky, punk?' So now I say to you, 'do you feel lucky'?" André looked from the gun to the eyes of the man holding it. He knew instantly that this man was not a shopkeeper; it was not the actions but the eyes that told the story. André understood that this shopkeeper had just killed a man and had not had the slightest compulsion about it. André had seen two people die today. He had believed he was cut out for this business, but now he felt his bowels grow hot and loose, and a gagging sensation filled his mouth.

"No, I don't." He felt the cramp in his stomach, as if someone had hit him, hard.

"You play at this, but you have not seen many people die, have you?" Jean Philippe said while motioning for André to open his coat and remove the weapon. Andre' complied without comment.

"It was not supposed to be this way." André dropped his large semi-automatic pistol to the floor.

"It is never how you imagine it. It is not like the movies or television. When people die, they are dead for a long time. Do you smell that?" Jean Philippe motioned with the gun toward Teo on the floor.

"Yes, it's awful" André replied.

"Yes, it is. When he died his sphincter muscle let go and he crapped all over himself. If you look carefully, you would probably also notice that he ejaculated as he died. It often happens, but you have never seen it, have you?" Jean Philippe pointed to the chair for the other man to sit down in. André had turned a terrible color, a mixture of gray and green. He suddenly leaned forward and vomited into his own hands, the pinkish white mixture cascading down his leg and onto his shoes and the floor.

"You are not very good at this business, my friend, and that is good for you." Jean Philippe reached behind him, grabbed a rag and tossed it to the man, to aid in his self esteem more than his cleaning up.

"You never protested your innocence or screamed for help or tried to make me think you came here for any other reason than to do me harm. That is mistake number one. Mistake two, is carrying a weapon in a holster. That is a dead giveaway that you are something official, cop, investigator, but more than likely some kind of asshole spy. Now if you are very careful, you will not make mistake number three." Jean Philippe leaned against the doorway and lowered the weapon to the side of his leg, out of sight of any passer-byes.

"What is mistake number three?" The words had a moist sound as André coughed.

"Not answering every question I ask you in a precise fashion with a lot of explanation attached."

"Or else?" André tried to hold on to some of his bravado. He tried telling himself that he had to get out of this and report back. What is he going to tell those who asked what happened here tonight? André was way out of his depth and knew it.

"Look at yourself, then look at that piece of shit bleeding all over my floor. Do you think I give a good Goddamn about you, or him? Are you some kind of whacked-out cowboy that thinks after all this that you are going to beat me and get answers out of me?" Jean Philippe raised the MAB and fired one round directly into André's kneecap, it shattered; the bullet tore through ligaments and tendons exiting the back of his leg, and spending its energy into the floor. Andre' screamed and fell into the vomit on the floor. He was crying and clutching his bleeding kneecap.

"Do you think this is some kind of mystery writer's game? Now who are you and who do you work for?"

Jean Philippe walked closer and looked down at the man on the floor.

"I am a member of the Swiss Guard and I work for the Vatican." André was weaving in and out of consciousness; he could feel the warm stream of blood oozing under him.

"Who in the Vatican?"

"I can't tell you that!" Andre' was trying to keep some control.

Jean Philippe put the muzzle of the gun over the open wound and pushed down. André let out a scream and sucked it back when Jean Philippe took the pressure away.

"Who?"

"Archbishop Giovanni, the Office of Special Congregations. Please don't hurt me anymore."

André felt himself getting cold. He especially noticed it around his abdominal area.

"I won't hurt you anymore, but I think it is too late, the bullet hit an artery and you've lost too much blood."

Jean Philippe walked back over and looked at the other man. He pulled the Diplomatic Passport from Teo's pocket and examined it. Then walked back and looked down at the other man. André had slipped into the blackness that comes from the loss of blood to the brain, and would be dead in a few moments.

Jean Philippe knew he should feel something different, something he used to feel long ago. But if things were different and he was tied to a chair and they were pouring mercury down his throat, would they have had any regrets or feeling of human compassion for him?

"Not likely!" He spoke to the room in general. He walked to the phone and called a number he had to sometimes use. There would be two men around in a few minutes to tidy up the place. The voice on the other end suggested that he should be gone, a late dinner perhaps, or a evening at the cinema. Jean Philippe looked at his watch and decided he needed to be back by midnight. He certainly had some interesting information for his friend. He stood for an appreciative moment while the finale of the Opus 22 float through the room.

CHAPTER FOURTEEN

*"When that which is coming comes - and no soul shall then deny its coming
- some shall be abased and others exalted."*
Holy Koran - Book of That Which is Coming

Jacob sat looking at the stack of material on his desk. He knew more about this man than he could have dreamed two days before and yet he still did not have the answers to the two most vital of questions: What does Abdul have that is so valuable? And where is he? Jacob knew that without this information, all of the rest of the information meant nothing. It was two in the morning as he sat wondering what this game was all about. It was midnight in central Europe. Things were still happening, but he felt like a blind man in a fight. He could swing like anything, but that did not mean he would strike his opponent.

It had been three hours since anything important had come in. Oh, he had been given some more background information from his field agents, but nothing relevant to the issue at hand. He decided to walk down to the basement to see who was in the situation room. It was an old habit, but he hated to just sit there and stare at the wall.

Jacob went down the back staircase and passed the guard at the security desk, who was reading the latest copy of the *Jerusalem Post*. He put the paper down when he saw Jacob approach.

"It is okay, Avi, if I were sitting down here I would be doing a cross-word puzzle." Jacob joked.

"Oh, I've already done that," the security officer looked at his watch, "it took me about thirty-five minutes."

They both laughed and Jacob walked into the room filled with computers and tape recorders. The lights were low, but that is the way most of the people liked it. They were called the "Mole People." They never knew if it was day or night, and most of them looked as if they had never seen sunlight. The "Vampire Chamber," Hiram used to call it, not because of the darkness, but because keeping it running sucks a lot of money from the budget.

Jacob thought about the way operations use to be done, as he looked at this Electronics Warfare Center, for that is what it was, and he knew he would not go back to the old days for anything. This new technology was the wave of the future and it would only increase. These people would eventually run the intelligence service with satellite imagery, computer hacking, telephone tapping, and the ability to compare and contrast thousands of bits of apparently unrelated information in a matter of minutes. He knew he would not understand as much as he did about the present situation without the people in this room and their constant communication with the agents in the field. He thought about the times he had waited in some alley to meet some low-life and pay him for scraps of information that half the time somebody else had already found in a newspaper. No, he did not regret the improvements that had come to his profession.

Jacob waited for the supervisor to get off the telephone. "I was getting bored up there, anything new?"

The agent looked at his desk and pulled a file with perhaps seven or eight sheets of handwritten notes. "Yes, I got confirmation as you walked in. It just arrived." The man read the sheet again to make sure of the details.

"Well. . ." Jacob felt irritated having to wait for something that might be important.

"I am not completely sure, but the description matches. The agent that called it in thinks that your man Senor Lindquist is on the 1:00 A.M. flight from Athens to Istanbul. He is traveling under his own identity. We tapped the airlines computer terminal and he shows up on the manifest, but no confirmation yet whether he will be on the flight." The man dropped that sheet and picked up another.

"Also, it seems the list you wanted of the Swiss Guards was obtained and copies were sent to Paris. Two of the guards on the list fit the description of the men involved in the shooting of the old woman earlier today, if that means anything." The phone rang and the agent turned to pick it up.

"Mean anything! Good God, this is what I have been waiting for!" He was talking to the man's back. He spoke a few words, hung up and turned back to Jacob.

"What was that?"

"Nothing, never mind." Jacob thought for a minute, then picked up a pad and started to write.

"These are the next set of orders. I need a Rapid Response Team in Istanbul by seven in the morning; I don't care if you have to call the army, get them there. I want two agents each from Athens, Paris, and Madrid on planes tonight. Everyone will meet at Joseph Ben Gasum's place at seven. Give them directions, papers; they can use anything they need, but I want them there. Everyone is to be armed. Call the embassies and have all of them given diplomatic papers, from whatever country they need to use. Pull out all the stops, but get them moving, now!"

Without waiting for a response Jacob turned and walked back upstairs. He called the security officer at the front desk and told him to arrange for the private jet and some kind of cover story. He wanted the jet fueled and ready at the airport in thirty minutes. Jacob also wanted two members of the security service with him.

Jacob pulled an overnight case out of the closet in the office, and was packed and heading for the door in less than three minutes. He wanted to be in Istanbul before that flight landed. He mused to himself, "now I get to see what Abdul the Bandit looks like when he's dressed up and acting civilized." The car was waiting at the front door with two young and very tough looking men holding the door open.

**

At midnight Abdul picked up the payphone in the Athens airport. He inserted the phone credit card he had just purchased at the airport store and dialed Jean Philippe's number in Paris. It rang three times and then the bass voice came on the line.

"Oui."

"I am taking in the night life of the Old World."

"Sounds wonderful right now."

"Did you have any luck in finding out who our friends are?"

"Who they *were*." Jean Philippe was quiet for a moment so Abdul could change the tense of his words.

"Do we know who they were?"

"Oui. They belonged to the Swiss Guard. They worked for someone named Giovanni, the Archbishop of the Office of the Special Congregation."

Silence filled the space between the two men as Abdul digested this. Nearly a minute of dead air ticked by.

"Okay, now I know. I am heading for Istanbul."

"Do you need me?"

"It would be safer for you if you did not come."

"I don't think so."

"Why?"

"Because tomorrow at roll-call, the Swiss Guards are going to be missing two of their finest."

"Permanently?"

"Oui."

"Bad?"

"I have had better days." Jean Philippe betrayed nothing in his voice, but Abdul knew this incident would hang heavy, as it had in the past. Jean Philippe did not like this kind of action. He could do it, because he was trained for it, but that did not make it any easier.

"The Continental Hotel."

"Oui."

"I will reserve a room for you under the name Lindquist."

"Tomorrow. Stay alive, I want to know what you have gotten me into."

"Reasonable request."

"The package?"

"Leave it there for right now."

The line went dead and Abdul hung up. He was watching the crowd around him, and he did not notice anything that would raise his suspicions, which fact itself raised a lot. Possibly he was paranoid, but then again, being paranoid doesn't mean that someone is not out to get you.

As he moved toward the boarding gate, Abdul found a restroom and changed from his street clothes into the cassock he carried in his valise. He combed his hair back and put on a pair of black heavy framed glasses. It was not much of a change but he hoped it was enough to catch somebody off guard.

***

The young man entered the darkened room; a single lamp was burning on the large desk. The old man sat there reading one of a hundred documents lying on top of a stack in front of him. The older man fondled the beads. On the desk sat an untouched cup of tea that had grown cold hours before. The younger man leaned down and whispered, "It is as you had said. The proof will be established on Wednesday."

The older man reached out and touched the other's hand. "May God see us through this, Thomas."

"He is all we have now."

"In truth He is all we ever have. Thank you. Go to bed now and I will see you in the morning."

"Good night."

***

Father Leno sat at his desk and went through the list again. Where could they be? They had missed the nine o'clock check-in call. It would be disagreeable to have to tell that bastard he had lost two agents in Paris. He looked at his list again and tried to figure out how he could cover this deficiency in staffing. The Papal Guards were already stretched to the breaking point. If he had to pull two more off duty, he might as well hire private security guards to protect St. Peter's. He picked up the phone and called the exchange office in Paris.

CHAPTER FIFTEEN

"The man who knows not and knows not that he knows not, is a fool
- shun him,
The man who knows not and knows that he knows not, is a child - teach
him,
The man who knows and knows not that he knows, is asleep - awaken
him,
The man who knows and knows that he knows is wise- follow him"
A Five Thousand Year old Sanskrit saying found on the Temple of Kali
in India.

The flight from Athens got in late. It arrived at the gate at 4:34 A.M., local time. The usual groups were there to meet their loved ones and friends returning home. Businessmen hurried through customs hoping to get a cab at the street side of the concourse that would quickly get them to their hotels. They wanted a few hours sleep, a shave, a clean shirt and tie, whatever it would take for them to make their careers more secure with the new deal they had been working on. Some visitors arrived dressed in vacation clothing; then there were the few ordinary passengers just wanting to get out of the airport.

Abdul cleared customs with no great difficulty. He had his single valise and the story that he was visiting one or two libraries to conduct research. The bored customs officer looked at his passport and did not even bother comparing the photo to the man. He stamped it and made some obligatory statement under his breath about having a good day and waved Abdul through in hopes that his endless line would soon be empty.

Abdul walked down the side of the concourse and scanned the crowd for any faces that might stand out. He did not notice the older man with the heavy lips and brow who moved in beside him to match his steps.

"Good morning, Father Lindquist, or should I say Abdul?"

Abdul tightened and half turned to the man. "Do I know you, sir?"

"No, not at all. . . but I know you. I know a great deal about you and I think that we should have a little talk."

Abdul noticed the two men that fell in behind them, both young and hard. He looked around the airport that was very quiet at this time of the morning.

"I must beg off, sir. I am very tired and need to get back to the other Brothers of the community. I am sure it would be interesting, but I believe that you have made a mistake." Abdul moved his valise to his left hand.

"No, I haven't made a mistake, nor do I want you to make any mistakes either. I want to talk to you, but if you think you can get away because we are in a public place, please forget that notion. These two men have orders that if you try to escape, they must shoot you down as you run." Jacob turned in front of the other man and blocked his path. "We want to do this quietly and with as little attention as possible, for both of our sakes."

"I am sure you mean well, but I don't know what you are talking about, I can assure you." Abdul dropped into a crouched position and landed the first kick directly into the man closest behind him; his valise came up from the floor and smashed into the second man's head, which was between the valise and the concrete wall. He then threw an elbow backwards that hit Jacob directly on the nose. Blood flew as the older man hit the ground. Abdul sprinted around a corner in less than two seconds. The action had been so quick that no one had a chance to respond. He passed one of the policemen guarding the front door and told him that someone had tried to mug an old man around the corner. The policeman ran and turned the corner where he stopped the younger man who was in pursuit of Abdul. He threw him against the wall and held him there until the other officer arrived. It was only seconds until all three of the Israeli agents were trying to explain what they were doing. Abdul was leaving in a cab before he looked at his closed hand, and the older man's wallet, which he had taken. Going through it, Abdul found a press card, two credit cards and a driving permit from Syria. It also had a photo of an attractive woman, inscribed "Shalom, Ann" on the back

Abdul sat back in the seat of the cab. He realized that someone else had entered the game, the Mossad. He closed his eyes and sighed. This was going to be more difficult than he thought. Now he had to find a way to slip through an opening that was closing from two sides. If agents were here from Israel, they must know about the package. They would not be very happy, because of tonight's little adventure. He knew the next time they would come better prepared and ready to draw first blood. Tonight he had been lucky, but his gut told him not to trust too much in luck. It had a way of running out.

CHAPTER SIXTEEN

"Do they not see how we have given them a sanctuary of safety,
while all around them men are carried off by force?
Would they believe in falsehood and deny God's goodness?"
Holy Koran - Book of the Spider

"You have the top brass from the Vatican on a private jet heading your way. They have at least ten Swiss Guards with them. We are talking the top guy in the Office of Special Congregations, his two right-hand 'yes men' and a secretary. They should be on the ground sometime tonight and it looks like they are not staying at the Church Residency in Istanbul, but at some prince's palace on the hill." The voice from Rome was hollow and empty. Jacob had talked to him before and knew he was one of the Mossad's people, but had never met him.

"How did you get this information?" Jacob felt his face flush before he finished the sentence.

"A little bird told me; a pigeon to be exact." The voice never changed in its tenor.

"Tell the little bird that Jacob is sending some bird seed for it."

"That is always helpful." The line went dead.

Jacob had asked for certain calls to be redirected to his cell phone number and this was one of them. He was now starting to buy information. He did not know what this meant, but it had something to do with Abdul and the package. This time Jacob was not going to let arrogance and stupidity, get in his way. He called in five of the members of the Rapid Response Team that spoke Arabic and Turkish like natives and directed them to follow the group that was going to land in the private jet. "Get close, but don't let them know that they are being watched. Report back to me personally when they have arrived at their final destination." Jacob knew if he watched them closely enough, he would probably find Abdul.

It was Tuesday afternoon and he wanted to sleep for a while. He gave orders for the duty officer to wake him if anything important came up. Then he drifted into a quiet sleep, sitting up right in the chair next to the window. The afternoon air that flowed in from the Bosporus was sweet and heavily laded with salt.

***

Jean Philippe told Abdul that he would walk through the old bazaar and check out the place where the meeting was to occur tomorrow. He walked for an hour and a half then stopped at a small café. Ordering coffee and a small roll, Jean Philippe sat and watched the people pass by. He replayed the conversation in his head a half dozen times. What had the man who called him last night meant, that if he failed nothing would change? He had gone over and over it in his mind. He had to make a compromise, something Jean Philippe did not do well. Finishing his coffee, he made his decision. Jean found a small tobacco shop with a public telephone and dialed the number from a slip of paper he carried. He had written it backwards, as he always did; it was not much of a security measure, but he felt if anyone got it off his body, it wouldn't really matter at that point. In fact, more power to them if they figured it out. The phone rang a half a dozen times. Then a voice answered.

"This is me." He spoke quickly. "Yes, that's right. I am not going to talk very long, so just listen. He is in Istanbul, and I am with him. However, there is something not right about all of this." He paused and listened.

"Of course, I have the package. I thought you knew that."

Jean Philippe looked around the bazaar for faces that were watching him, but saw none.

"No, I did not open the package. The man is a master of explosives. If it blew up in my face, he would know that he could not trust me. The package might not even be what you are looking for. He could have just given me an explosive device and hidden the package elsewhere."

Jean Philippe listened again. "No, there is something else. I am not sure, but I know that tomorrow it will be over." He let phone hang down for a minute while he lit a cigarette. He picked the phone back up. "Yes, I'm still here. We are staying at the Continental. . . third floor. Yes, I will call if I can." He hung up and left the bazaar.

***

An Arab beggar was sitting next to the doorway of the brass shop when Jean Philippe walked past. He paid no attention to the man in the

94

blue robe sitting on the ground holding his bowl out. A couple of German tourists walked by and dropped a few coins in the beggar's cup and continued to take in the sights of the old bazaar.

Abdul sat there and watched for the forty-five minutes that it had taken for Jean Philippe to wrestle with his thoughts and finally make the call. After Jean passed by, Abdul got up, brushed himself off, and walked with an affected limp up the street towards the center of the bazaar. He needed time to sort out the ever-shrinking noose tightening around his neck.

He had known Jean Philippe for years and had on more than one occasion placed his life in the man's hands. It was difficult to believe Jean Philippe would betray him. But then again, there was always Judas — nobody would have believed he could have betrayed anyone either.

CHAPTER SEVENTEEN

*"As for those that have faith and do good work,
We shall not deny them their reward."*
Holy Koran - Book of the Cave

Hiram sat in his office and wondered what was happening in Istanbul. He hadn't heard from Jacob since last night before he left. Jacob thought they would be able to acquire Abdul and get him back to headquarters without incident. If he had not checked in, Hiram knew that something had gone wrong with the plan. He understood this meant a great deal to all of them, but he had trusted Jacob so long that he was not going to try to second guess Jacob at this point. He was trying to organize his papers and get rid of thirty years of memories in his desk when the phone rang.

"Yes." He listened to the voice at the other end.

"Yes I am."

He took his pen out and made some notes. "This is quite unusual, isn't it?"

The voice continued and then, suddenly, Hiram sat back in his chair.

"Of course I understand, but it is a little late for this. I have people on the ground, and I would image they are none too happy about any of this. If what you say is true, I need to get in contact with them and do some explaining." The voice at the other end continued.

"At once. I will go there myself."

Hiram sat and listened some more, then covered his eyes with his hands. He did not believe what he was hearing.

"I will be there in three hours. Thank you, Mr. Prime Minister." He put down the phone and picked up the interior line that rang the situation room. It took two rings to be picked up.

"Has Jacob called in?"

"He did, about an hour or so ago for updates." The officer sitting on the situation desk was emotionless and matter of fact.

"Get to him. Tell him to do nothing until I am there. He is to meet me at the airport in about two and a half hours. Get the airplane ready for me also."

"That's not my responsibility, sir. That is logistics."

"Do you know to whom you are speaking?"

"Yes sir."

"Just do it. I don't have time to explain. . . understand?"

"Yes, I will call and take care of it, right away."

Hiram walked across the hall and tapped gently on the ADI's door and then entered. The ADI was sitting going over a stack of printouts that were covered with figures. "Hold the fort for me. I will be gone for about two days."

"You can't. We have a meeting with the Knesset this afternoon."

"Deal with it, postpone it, lie to them, go yourself, but don't make too big a fool out of yourself. Just deal with it. I have more important business to handle."

"For instance?"

"Nothing that concerns you. I need to save a man from making a grave mistake." With that Hiram walked down the hallway. He was still rubbing his hands together, assimilating the information that he had just been told. Now if he could only make it, before all of this went awry, he would be grateful to his God.

***

Abdul was back in the room when Jean Philippe entered carrying his traveling case. He tossed it upon the bed without speaking. He looked at Abdul sitting by the window. Abdul had a faraway look in his eyes; he was on a different landscape, a long way from here. Jean Philippe had known this man a long time, and knew that he was a man of many moods, but when he got very quiet, he knew that something had caused him to search the corners of his mind for answers to unspoken questions.

"Are you all right?" Jean Philippe asked.

"No! I am tired, old, and can't remember the last time I closed my eyes without seeing the haunting faces of a hundred people that are now all dead. I find that my world grows smaller and smaller with each day. I wonder if at some moment in the past, I'd call it the 'defining point,' if at that moment I made the right choice. I believe that each of us is given the opportunity to choose a pathway, from hundreds of options. As we get older, these options decrease, until we reach that moment that is the defining point. It is that choice that defines who we are as people. We will be better than we could be, or worse than we should be; the terrible part about it is the fact that we make that decision with less than perfect information. Some of us make our choices early in life; others wait until the last possible moment, and then commit ourselves. But we never know if we are right or wrong until much later, at a point when there is no turning back. Mostly when there are no more "graduations" on our horizons."

Jean Philippe turned in his chair to face the other man. "This business has been too much for you. You have been at it too long and alone too much." Jean Philippe knew the truth of his words, but he was speaking as much for himself as for Abdul.

"I don't know. I only believe that this thing must be seen through to the finish, no matter how terrible it becomes."

"You frighten me when you speak that way." Jean Philippe moved over to the bed and lit a cigarette.

"You? Afraid? I can't believe that. I have never seen you with fear. We have been in places that most people would not want to imagine and yet you are always a pillar." Abdul looked at the other man. He wanted to ask all the questions that were in his mind, but feared the answers. If he found out that his old friend was now capable of betrayal, then he had lost the anchor, the last reference point to any humanity he had ever known.

Jean Philippe whispered, "I am afraid all the time. I fear for what I have become, and I fear for you. I fear that someday all of this, what I have done and am doing will overcome me and I will stand there naked before whatever I think is my God and have to explain what it is that I have done, and why. It seems as if I should have finished the seminary and found a small parish to spend my life in and die quietly, being loved and admired by the people I served. But that has not been my road, or yours."

Abdul thought he could see tears brimming in Jean Philippe's eyes. He had never seen so deeply into his friend and yet was never so scared of him as at that moment.

"What do you need? I was just sitting here trying to play through what tomorrow would bring."

Abdul tried to reverse the flow of the river in his mind and bring them both back up to the level that they needed to be, if they were to function and get this job done.

"I presume that you did not bring our Colt with you." Jean Philippe was opening his case, the inside of which was empty.

"I left it and the Walther in a locker in Athens. I could not get it on the plane and was not about to try."

"That is what I thought would be the case before I left Paris, so I brought my special traveling case. It was built about five years ago, for a customer that never picked it up. It has very small lead-lined sides, so that the guns and ammunition fit into it and will not be detected by the airport radar screening systems for passengers. It takes a lot to notice the indentations on the side and for the most part the average security guard would miss it. It is just a heavy case to them filled with underclothes and a shaving kit."

Jean Philippe popped the sides out and exposed two compartments that held two heavy-framed automatic pistols and three extra clips of ammo for each gun.

"Genius!" Abdul picked up one of the guns and felt its weight and handling characteristics.

He took the extra clips and checked the level of the ammo in each of them. "This will at least offer us some form of equalization if things go wrong tomorrow."

"There will be more help also." Jean Philippe busied himself with checking the weapons and did not look up.

"What do you mean?" Abdul had that strange sensation that he was about to tap dance on thin ice and learn the coldness of the water beneath.

"I called in a favor. I called someone that I think can help. Whatever this is about, we cannot do it alone. Not if you know that we are up against at least two groups, maybe more. We needed a little insurance and I bought it for us." Jean Philippe sat back and smiled. "You were not going to ask me about the telephone call, were you?"

"What telephone call?" Abdul continued to wear his game face.

"The one I made this morning from the bazaar, the one you know I made. The one you watched me make." Jean Philippe let his face go to its nature gloomy appearance.

"How did you know?"

"I knew. Because you have reached a point to where you can trust no one, not even me. You have been in-country too long and you believe that everything and everyone are siding against you. You have gone native, old friend. You are more comfortable wearing the robes of a Bena Salla Arab than you are in the robes of your church. But it is interesting. I sat there and watched as the whole scene around continued to change, with the exception of the beggar that was not begging enough." Jean Philippe looked at his friend with pity and remorse. "Do you think I would sell you out? Or is it that this thing you do is so important that nothing else matters anymore? Not Jasmine's life, nor mine. Does anything matter?"

"Yes." The words were choked out and hung between the two men.

Jean Philippe sat there and watched the internal hell that this man was going through. He could only image what great secret he held and what was driving him on. The silence wrapped itself around the two men like a shroud.

Jean Philippe got up and closed the case. He walked from the room without another word and Abdul sat there looking at the faded roses on the carpet. All he could think was "when will this eternal penitence be done?" He got up and walked to the window. Who had Jean Philippe called and would they help or just become one more hurdle in the middle of the track that he must find a way over. He thought this would be the best way to cover a lie, with another lie. If he were Jean Philippe, and believed he had been caught, he would have done the same thing? Fake it by admitting to the call and then tell the story that it was really for their own protection? Abdul held his head with his hands. Could nothing ever be just what it appeared to be? Unfortunately, history had proven to him that it was seldom that simple.

***

Giovanni had explained every detail of the meeting to his assistants. Both priests understood their roles during the meeting. One of the priests was to photograph everything that he could. The other was to keep the Swiss Guards informed by radio of the progress of the meeting and actions they might need to take. Giovanni was emphatic that they must never lose sight of him or Abdul from the time the meeting began. After the exchange was made, he would keep Abdul under surveillance until the package was delivered to him personally. He knew that this man was dangerous beyond all belief, but he felt he now had enough people with him to complete the task. He needed that package. His time schedule was now three weeks behind where should be, and that was not good. If his plan was to work, he needed the next forty-eight hours to go without any additional problems. He would deal later with Abdul; he was sure of that. But right now, it was necessary to get the package and get back to Rome.

Prince al-Rashid entered his apartment in the huge old building. He walked over to the Archbishop and sat in one of the red leather chairs by the desk.

"How goes this thing?" The man was dark, corpulent and bejeweled. He was wearing the robes of an old time sultan, something in which he took great pleasure. Whenever he left his home he wore the typical raiment's of a modern businessman, but in his own home, he played the part of the Middle Eastern potentate of another century.

"We will know tomorrow. All that I do know right now is that if I cannot complete this thing soon, many of us will be unhappy." Giovanni's hard eyes looked at the other with concern.

"We knew this was a dangerous enterprise before we started, but what choice did we have? If we do not act now, none of us will have our dreams, will we?" He drummed his fat fingers on the desk.

"Dreams! 'Desires' is more the word! Desires for those things that we believe belong to us. You desire your lands back, which were taken from your family fifty years ago. I desire to be Pope of the greatest church on earth. Our other friends want to stay in the shadows and not have their worlds disturbed." He closed his notebook and sat back, looking at the tapestry on the wall.

"From the time I first entered the church, I realized what great powers the Pope could use, but for the most part never has, not in five centuries. I want that power!"

"What will you do with it if you do get it — change the world?"

"Oh, yes. Change a large part of it. By the time I am through, they will want to canonize me and make my name a household word in all Christian countries. . ." Giovanni's words were interrupted by the other man.

"Don't you mean in all Catholic countries?"

"No, actually. I believe when I am through, the only Christians will be Catholics." His words were heavy-stated with force and conviction.

"Another Counter Reformation in our current world! But how!?"

"The same way that we plan to reduce Israel to a memory." Before the other man could continue his questioning, Giovanni rose and bid him good day. He needed to check on his people.

The Prince was left sitting alone in the room. He sighed then heaved out of the chair. It was time to visit the prostitutes that he loving called his harem. He toddled down the corridor dreaming of the return to his homeland along the edge of the sea.

CHAPTER EIGHTEEN

"I say that on the side of the conspirator, there is nothing
but fear, jealousy and apprehension of punishment."
The Prince - Niccolo Machiavelli

Hiram's plane landed and he entered the country of Turkey under the protection of diplomatic immunity. He carried the papers of a diplomat assigned to the Egyptian Embassy in Istanbul. He knew that he would not be staying long, so using these documents would not raise the attention of anyone, at least not for a few days. Hiram had not gone on this type of mission in many years, having been deskbound has fit his rank. And since the onset of the illness, it had been even harder for him to get out into the field. His endurance was no longer there. He knew that this was probably the last flight he would take anywhere. But this was not the sort of matter he would talk to anyone over an open telephone line about, especially the old friend he had sent out to do his bidding. By now, other agencies would have detected the movement of so many agents into a concentrated area; they would have all their assets trying to find out the reason for the action. Hiram shuddered at the thought of the repercussions this action would cause in other capitals around the world, if they found out about it. The facts surrounding this case would not get out to the press or even to their own people. Abdul the Bandit was going to be an empty file if he had anything to do with it.

Jacob was waiting at the curb in front of the airport when Hiram arrived. They got into the rented car and the driver, without a word, headed for the safe house. They had just turned into one of the narrow lanes off the main motorway when Hiram spoke.

"Him?" He pointed to the driver.

"Saul. He has been with us for eight years, came over from the army. I trust him." Jacob knew that Hiram trusted no one. He had seen too many betrayals in all his years in the service of his country.

"Have you found Abdul?"

"We had him and I lost him. Two men were injured, one badly, but he will recover. I am sorry." Jacob looked out the car window at the garbage-lined streets with half-naked children playing in the dirt.

"Looks as if you also got a pummeled." Hiram turned while lighting his cigarette and looked at the side of Jacob's face.

"Yes," he said with a sigh, "he got me also, but that favor will be returned. . . I promise you."

"No, it won't." Hiram rolled down the window part way.

"What do you mean? You can't mean you are pulling me off of this? I need . . . I want to finish this. It is important. . ."

"Enough! I am still your boss, and if I remember correctly you still take orders from me!" Hiram looked ahead at the turn the driver was making up the hill, into a worse section of town than they had just passed through.

"Yes sir, of course. . . but. . ." Jacob was showing his frustration.

"But, nothing, you have new orders. I had to bring them myself because I couldn't believe them when I heard them." Hiram flipped the stub of his cigarette out the window.

"What are the new orders?"

Hiram ignored his question, which only provoked Jacob that much more. "How many people do you have here on the ground and available right now?"

"Fourteen, including myself." Jacob knew he would not get the information until Hiram was ready to give it.

Hiram and Jacob rode in silence for about ten more minutes, until they pulled into the garage beneath an old crumbling house. They went in through the garage door and Saul went up to where the other men waited for instructions. Hiram and Jacob walked out onto the deck that overlooked this part of the city. The view was a jumble of electrical wires and television antennas. The sky was brown with haze and smog. "Great place, you must have spent months finding this hole." The bitter sarcasm hung like bile in the air.

"You did not come all this way to make architectural commentaries on my choice of a safe house." Jacob found himself angrier than he could remember being in a long time. He wanted to know what brought this poor old dying man all the way here. "Hiram!"

"Enough, I know enough. It seems like we are fools. We know our business, but there are things that we do not know. The Prime Minister called and told me that we must do one thing only in the Abdul Hassan case." Before Hiram could finish Jacob interjected.

"How does he even know about this, yet? That stinking little ADI of yours must have told him that. . . about doing this!"

"Stop! Samuel didn't tell him anything. The Prime Minister learned about it from someone whom you will probably meet later. But for right now, you, Jacob, have only two responsibilities to carryout. The first is that you are to refocus your team on one task, and one task only. They must protect Abdul Hassan's life, even at the cost of the whole team, if necessary."

Jacob's jaw dropped. He tried to speak but nothing would come out. He turned away to hide his anger and disbelief.

"Secondly, it is your personal responsibility to stay by Abdul's side and go with him wherever he asks you to go and do whatever he asks you to do." Hiram was trying to keep his words flat, but he knew the affect they were having on his old friend.

"The man tried to kill me yesterday, he hurt two of my people and now you want me to be his wet nurse?" Jacob was purple with rage.

"No, I don't want you to. However, I am ordering you as a member of the government of Israel, to whom you swore an oath of allegiance, to follow the orders that your superior gives you, and without questioning the authority that stands behind them." Hiram found himself getting angrier by the minute. This is not the way he wanted this to happen, but time was of the essence and he had none left for debates, even with old friends.

"I understand. I will comply." Jacob felt as though he was twenty-one again and being dressed down by his captain in the tank regiment. He understood that something had shaken Hiram to the point that he was going to be exact and clear about these instructions, and that no one was going to make a mistake on his watch.

"Now, do you have any questions?" Hiram calmed down and lowered his voice.

"Why?"

"That will become evident in time. That is all that I can tell you right now. I need your man to get me back to the airport. I need to go home as soon as possible." He turned to find a place to sit down. Jacob helped him to the steps.

"You're sick!" Jacob sat down next to him.

"Jacob, I am dying, and this business has not helped me. But I promise you on your love for Ann, it is this important. I have one more thing to do when I get back to Israel and my career will be finished on this old ball of dust. Jacob . . . keep that man alive, whatever it takes. . . keep him alive."

Hiram slumped a little more.

"Come inside and rest for awhile, then I will take you back to the airport myself."

"No, there is no time for that. You need to get to Abdul as soon as possible and let him know that you are here to help." Hiram mopped his face with his handkerchief and blotted his mouth.

"Your man Saul is all I need to get me back to the plane."

"But we don't even know where Abdul is right now. We have been following the Catholics in hopes that they would lead us to him."

"He is at the Continental Hotel on the third floor; he is with a Frenchman, both are to be taken under your wing. Get to Abdul before he meets with the Catholics. Tell him who you are and what you are doing here. He will tell you more than I can."

"If he doesn't kill me on sight." Jacob felt his lip and remembered his last meeting with Abdul.

"Get to him today. I am not sure, but I think either tomorrow or the next day, things will be happening." Hiram got to his feet and dusted himself off. He turned and reached out for Jacob's hand.

"Good bye old friend. . . I may not be there when you get back."

"Nonsense, I shall be a couple of days, no more than that. I will be seeing you back home, soon."

Hiram and Jacobs eyes met, they both knew that this was probably a lie, but neither was going to make anything more out of it than this.

Jacob called Saul and gave him instructions. He watched as the car pulled away and down the hill back through the crowded suburb and out of sight. Jacob looked to the sky and wondered if he would ever know the truth.

CHAPTER NINETEEN

"Wealth and Children are the ornaments of this life."
Holy Koran - Book of the Cave

They moved in slowly, two by two. Each took a different route and all of them met on the third floor of the old hotel. Someone had bribed the deskman to tell them which rooms Abdul and Jean Philippe occupied. They had gone over the plan a half a dozen times and Jacob emphasized the object of this raid was to contact the targets, not to hurt them. He did not want any of his people injured or killed either, so he explained in great detail how truly dangerous this one man was. He was not sure of the Frenchman, but being in Abdul's company, he assumed that he was every bit as capable of causing great bodily harm as Abdul. This needed to be a quiet raid, what is known in the business as a snatch and grab, a kidnapping. Jacob had determined it would be best to take both of these men into custody before trying to talk to them. That meant going in and wrapping them up, taking them down the back staircase to the waiting cars, and then getting them back to the safe house. This he knew how to do well. Then when the men were restrained, he would talk to them and explain his position. This would take a ten-man team plus himself and all he knew was that it had to be quiet.

Jacob's team waited in the hallway while one of the agents unscrewed the light bulbs from the hallway sockets. By darkening the hallway Jacob's team gained an advantage. Each man had a pair of night vision goggles and a small wireless communications device. One of the men placed a listening device on each of the two doors to see if he could hear any sounds. He shook his head to the negative. It was 1:30 A. M. Wednesday morning when the doors exploded inwardly and five men jumped on each of the figures lying in their beds in their separate rooms. Each target quickly became alert, but not quickly enough. Before they knew what had happened, their hands were handcuffed, gags had been pushed into their mouths and black hoods were dropped over heads. The whole operation took less than twenty seconds from start to finish. Jacob's team half-dragged, half-carried the men down the staircase and tossed them into the waiting cars. Inside, their legs locked together with nylon speed cuffs, the types used on packages. The captives were placed on the floorboards and two men in the backseat of each car used their feet on them to hold them in place. The three cars then raced from the old quarter of town, through light traffic toward the safe house.

***

The young man walked into the room. In the semi-darkness he could see the figure of the older man sitting in his high back chair sleeping. He started to leave without awakening him, but was stopped by the voice that came out from under the heavy fur blanket that covered the other man.

"You don't have to go if you have something to say, or if you need me. You know that."

"I didn't want to disturb you; I know how late you worked and how much you need your sleep."

"I will be sleeping for a long time, soon. Come closer and sit by me, please."

The younger man went over and sat on the footstool indicated. "Now tell me what keeps you up so late tonight?"

"The Israelis have made contact, but something strange happened. It looks as if they kidnapped both men." The young man sat quietly.

"How do we know this?"

"We have had them watched since Msgr. Baptiste called in earlier today."

"Does Giovanni know anything about this yet?"

"No, only our men there and you."

"Let us see if we have allies now or not. Thank you and good night."

"Good night Your Holiness." The young man walked quietly out of the Papal apartments. The Pope turned on the light next to his chair. He sat there considering the actions taken. He got up and walked over to the telephone where he dialed three digits and listened.

"Your Holiness, what may I do for you?"

"Father Leno, have you finished the special project I asked you to undertake?"

"Yes Your Holiness, we have it all, route and destination, code and encryption key. All of it."

"Bring it all up here if you will. I need to see it."

There was a minor hesitation then Leno answered, "Immediately Your Holiness."

The task was complete; now the Pope knew it was only the cleaning up of events that would matter. He knew that he had done something that no other Pontiff had done in ten centuries, but it did not please him. The cost had been great. Now he would pray for some men, who God in his goodness would come to their aid.

***

Abdul was sitting in a hard backed chair when his hood was taken off and the gag pulled from his mouth. His throat was dry and he could still taste the rag. A single light bulb burned directly in front of him. He could not see past the light, the same way all interrogations usually started. Normally they got a lot worse from here on. He knew his legs had been tied to the chair by nylon slip cords and his handcuffs were also connected to the chair. This limited all of his actions, and whoever was doing this knew their business.

Abdul turned to see if he could see anything in the room. Sitting next to him, Jean Philippe still had his hood on. This caught him off-guard. Normally you only question one man at a time, unless you are planning to shoot both of them at the same time. Abdul sighed, he had the feeling that he had come to the end of it, and that he was not going to walk away from this one.

A puff of smoke came out from behind the light and the head of a man in the middle ground between darkness and light showed itself.

"The other, take his hood off." Someone pulled Jean Philippe's hood off and removed the gag from his mouth. He spat on the floor to clear his mouth of the residue of the rag.

"I am sorry for this treatment, but since our last meeting, I thought it best to try to control the environment. Otherwise we might have the same kind of misunderstanding as before." Jacob pulled a chair up so that he was directly across from both men. "And I can't afford that again. I am too old to be swapping blows with lads like you." He turned and spoke to someone behind him, "give them a drink of water, please." Hands reached into the light with water to clean their mouths and soothe their throats.

Jean Philippe immediately went into his act. "Can I have a cigarette? I am a French citizen and have only come here to see the Museum. I want to learn about recorders and how they were built in the seventeenth century. You must have made a mistake." Someone handed him a smoke, which he pulled in deeply.

"We know who both of you are and we are here to help you."

Abdul started to laugh. . . he in fact roared. "You are going to help us? I can see that you are sure as hell helping us right now. I have seen Christmas geese tied up less securely. Who is this French pig next to me? I don't know him. Get this pig eating son of a whore away from me!"

"Enough, Father Lindquist, we know who you are and that your friend, Monsignor Baptiste, is by your side to aid you. Or should I call you Abdul the Bandit?" Jacob sat back and looked at the men, both hard and who were marked with several scars. He shuddered because he had known men like this his whole life, hard, resilient, disciplined men who could take as good as they gave without a whimper or a cry. He felt strangely, that he was almost looking into the mirror of his own soul.

"I am Jacob Isaac and I work for an Intelligence Agency in Israel. My orders are to make sure that nothing happens to either of you. I am placing you under my protection for that purpose. This is on the order of my government." He waited.

"Then untie us." Abdul looked directly at the man.

"Not until you understand that we are going to need to work together on this. You cannot make this meeting with the Catholics without us being there. We cannot let either of you get hurt in this adventure."

"You're serious?"

"It would be much easier to put a bullet in your brain, than what we have to do." Jacob turned and spoke in Hebrew to his men. The lights came up in the room. There were half a dozen hard young men standing around. "Untie them and take the handcuffs off."

The men followed Jacob's instructions and Abdul rubbed his wrist and looked at Jean Philippe, who just shrugged in an expression of non-comprehension.

"Give them their guns and the extra clips." Hesitantly Abdul and Jean Philippe were handed the tools of their trade. They inspected the guns. They were in good working order and loaded.

"Now do you believe me?" Jacob had a pretty good idea how the scene would play out. Abdul pointed the gun at Jacob and looked at him for a long minute.

"What if we just opened up and shot all of you where you stand?" Abdul spoke and Jean Philippe got up to move slightly away.

"Then you would be losing our assistance and that of the state of Israel. Whatever it is that you are planning to do here in Istanbul, I think you may need us and our guns." Jacob never flinched as he spoke, but inside he was shaking with fear.

"Pretty cool customer is all I have to say for you, Mr. Isaac. But I want to know — how you know what we are here to do?"

"We figured it out. And we came to kill you if necessary, to keep you from giving the package to the Catholics. Then everything changed, and not one of us knows why. So it seems that someone knows more than we do, and they are willing to gamble on you, so. . ." He stood and walked up close to Abdul, "either shoot me now and get it over with, or come downstairs and explain to us what we are supposed to do." With that Jacob walked over to the door and opened it. He turned and looked at Abdul and Jean Philippe. Jean Philippe still had his weapon at the ready. Abdul motioned for him to put it away and placed his own in the back of his waistband. He walked across the room and then said, "Does anybody here make coffee, 'cause I am so scared that I could sure use a cup to calm my nerves."

One of the other men laughed he put his gun back into a holster and nodded, "I make good coffee." The room emptied as each man went down the staircase to the first floor.

CHAPTER TWENTY

"Fear God, oh History, and afflict me no more. The sight of you has made me detest life and the cruelty of your sickle has caused me to love Death."
"History and the Nation" - Kahlil Gibran

Father Leno walked into the Papal Apartments and stood looking at the Vicar of Rome, the Supreme Head of the Catholic Church. The man looked physically old and worn by the years of responsibility he had shouldered. But looking into his clear blue eyes, one could instantly tell that the vitality and mental acuteness he had brought to his office was still there; only his body was now failing him. The Pope gestured to the chair next to his desk and Leno sat on the very edge, almost at attention.

"Sit back, Father and relax. Our days are too filled with problems for men who serve the same Master to be on guard here." Again the Holy Father gestured to the man and finally Leno relaxed a bit. He had not been up here very often although his duties were extremely important to the protection of the Pope and the City-State of the Vatican. He could count on one hand the times that he had ascended the full staircase from his basement office to this room. He had no pretensions about ever sitting in this room as his apartment. That thought was one he had never entertained. His life was one of service to the men that wore the *'white of power'* in the ancient citadel.

The Pope finished writing on a document and set it aside. He turned his full attention to Leno.

"Do you have the information that we need?"

As an answer, Leno handed the Pope a file. The older man opened it and started to read each entry. He set each sheet to one side and studied the next one until he was finished.

"This much? That is what it has grown to?" The Pope turned to Leno who was sitting there looking at the *Rafael* painting that graced the apartment wall.

"Yes, Your Holiness. They have compounded interest, brought in funds from other enterprises and made loans to some of the largest multinational corporations in the world. There would appear to be about a quarter of that amount lent to others, the location of which we do not know."

The Pope studied the one file that was filled with codes and transaction numbers.

"Will this give you access to it?"

"Your Holiness, I must state that I have never previously committed such a sin as this and that I fear for my soul." Leno leaned forward. His nature was one of a stern and tough parish priest that had climbed the ladder of Vatican politics but still was grounded in his faith.

"It is not you, my son, who needs to worry about his soul. You have served your church and your Pope exceptionally well, and I have little to offer as reward. But I need to know if you can move this money from where it is to another account in a different place, with this information?"

"Yes, Your Holiness, I can. With the code and the access numbers provided I can place all or part of it anywhere you want it." There was a slight tremor to his voice that gave away some hidden feeling that the Pope immediately perceived.

"Do you think that I am moving this to my account?"

"No, Holy Father, it is just that this is so irregular. I am at a loss to understand what is going on."

"That is understandable, Father. This whole business is not something in which the church should be involved. I will say in time you will learn the truth."

The Pope studied Father Leno's face. All he saw was a sincere man who served his church well. "This money represents millions of lives that have been offered to a dark and malevolent cause. It has been hidden from the church and the men who have sat in this chair. The money has been used by men not worthy of even touching the hem of your robe to gain power, destroy lives, and do a thousand other things that if seen in the light of day, you and I would find repulsive. Now the funds will go where they belong. That is all I can tell you now, but later after all of this is done, we will sit and I will tell you the whole story."

"Holy Father, I am yours to command. I need no explanation." Leno felt he had crossed a line of protocol that he would never have done consciously.

"Yes, but all men fear power, as we should. What I have asked you to do is something that openly we would admonish in others, but yet, we are left with few alternatives. How, by the way, did you get all this information?"

"I had the decorators and painters replaced with men that work for me. I planted bugs, listening devices, in all the offices. Wiretaps were placed on all the telephones, and all of the computers were re-routed through the main frame in the basement. I placed a hidden camera in the ceiling of the Archbishop's office and pointed it at his computer screen, and recorded every entry he made in his personal database." Leno looked at the Pope through his heavy glasses and blinked.

"Where did you learn to do all of this, surely not at seminary?" The Pope smiled one of his rare smiles.

"I am Sicilian, Holy Father. We all have relatives that are involved in some form or another of. . . shall we say, less than professional conduct." Leno looked innocently up at the *Rafael* painting again hoping that the Pope would not asked more questions about his activities.

"You asked relatives to do our dirty work?"

"Yes, Your Holiness."

"Were they paid well?"

"I paid them."

"Make a proper pay voucher out for services provided with a little extra and send it up to me for my signature. The workman is worthy of his hire. I see no reason why the church can not afford to make sure its friends are dealt with fairly." Father Leno nodded and let the statement hang in the air.

The Pope opened his desk and took out a small black notebook. He opened it to a page and tore it out. "Can you have those funds moved into this account, by 10:00 this morning?" The Pope handed to the other man the slip of paper. Leno looked at it and looked up at the Pope.

"It may be difficult because it is so much, but I will do everything that I can to accomplish this."

"When it is done, call me on my private line and tell me it has been completed. Father Leno. . . there is nothing right now more important to me than this. I cannot stress the importance without sounding melodramatic. . . but lives hang in the balance by this action."

Leno got up and closed the file. "It will be done, Your Holiness, if I have to call in the favors of all the Sicilians in Europe."

The Pope stood with difficulty and embraced Leno. "Thank you, my son. Be about your business now, but call the minute it is accomplished."

With that Leno walked out of the Holy Apartment. He descended the staircase passing six Cardinals that were going up to see the Pope. He thought that five o'clock in the morning was a strange time for a conclave, but this was turning into strange times.

***

Abdul sat in the rickety old chair in the small kitchen drinking a cup of thick, heavy, Turkish coffee. He watched each of the men as they positioned themselves around the room. The air was still tense, for no one but he was fully aware of the actions that needed to be taken. He looked at Jean Philippe and still wondered whom he had called. Somehow Abdul knew it was all related to these men sitting here with him. He considered the fact that he may have underestimated his old friend. It was something he knew he would not wish to repeat.

"So, here we are. What do we do?" Jacob sat down at the table and lit a cigarette. The blue smoke drifted around the room giving the group the appearance of a secret cabal.

Abdul remarked, "I need to get to a computer around noon. I need to stop at an apothecary in the Moslem section of town and 'we' need to be in the old bazaar at three this afternoon. From there on, we will have to improvise. Archbishop Giovanni will meet me, but he won't come alone. There will be anywhere from six to sixty Swiss Guards in plainclothes with him. All armed and wanting really badly to place my head on one of the spikes outside the gates of the Old City."

Abdul went back to his coffee. One of the other men said something in Hebrew to Jacob. He turned and nodded. The man left the room.

"We may have an advantage in this." Jacob turned as the subordinate re-entered the room with a file folder, which he laid in front of Jacob.

"How is that?" Jean Philippe looked quizzically at the older man.

"Because someone was good enough to provide us with a list and photos of all the Swiss Guards who have been put on special assignment to the Archbishop." He opened the folder and spread the contents on the old wooden table. The photos scattered with sixteen men's faces staring back at them from glossy black and white photographs.

"Eureka!" Abdul pointed to a couple of the photos.

"These two will not be there." Jean Philippe picked up the two photographs and handed them back to Jacob.

"You sound certain." Jacob looked at the Frenchman, who did not change expression.

"Yes. They will not be there."

"Fourteen then. . . unless the Archbishop has gotten replacements." Jacob turned back to the agent who had brought the file. The man shrugged his shoulders suggesting that he had no knowledge of replacements added to the operation.

"That is still a lot of people to cover." Abdul sat there looking at the faces of what should be considered some of the finest young men in the world, who knew nothing of this business, and had no reason to be involved. They were just the innocent victims of a strange turn of events that could leave them causalities of another undeclared war. He hated that part of all of this. Good men, just trying to do their jobs and not understanding what it was all about. So many times in so many places he had seen this same thing happen. He looked around the room and thought the same thing about the men who now surrounded him. He was the only one in the room who knew the truth and yet all of these dedicated souls were willing to give up their lives in belief that what they were doing was important. He stared at his hands and they started to shake again. He felt the vomit push up in his throat and the blackness in the depth of his brain crawling like a living thing into his conscious mind. He squeezed the cup in his hand with so much pressure that it suddenly shattered. No one moved, but every eye in the room was on the man sitting there looking at the floor which now had the mixture of broken cup shards and blood dripping from his left hand. Jean Philippe then turned and picked up a towel to hand to Abdul. He wrapped it around his hand and looked up at the inquiring eyes.

"This business is about money, power, greed, and a lot of dead bodies all over Europe. It is about a bunch of bottom-feeders that would sell their own daughters on the street to make a franc. It is about crimes of which none of you can even begin to understand, and it is about one man that wants somehow to make it all right. He knows that it can never be erased. But he believes that some of it can be stopped and something left behind that is finer and better for his passing this way." Abdul got up and looked around the room. "I did not ask for your help. I don't need it. I can do this thing alone if necessary. I do not want to be responsible for any of your

SEAN DAVID MORTON - WAYNE E. HALEY

deaths. Can you understand that?" He moved to the sink to get a glass of water. Jacob motioned to his people to leave the room, quietly.

"It is a heavy burden that you carry, Father Lindquist." Jacob sat and looked at the man's back. He suddenly had a new appreciation for this man, stirred by the fact that he hated himself more than anyone else could. Jacob knew that feeling well, since the time he was a soldier in the desert and all the time he had worked in intelligence. It was the cost of protecting something that you love, and the payment of dues that go with being on the frontline.

"Please. . . Please don't call me *'Father'*." Abdul did not turn.

"I ask your pardon. It was not meant with disrespect." Jacob spoke quietly.

"It was not taken that way. It is just that it has been too long and too much. . ." Abdul trailed off as he looked at the face in the glass window staring back at him. . . a hollow ghostlike countenance in the morning light.

"I need to get back to the hotel and make some arrangements." Abdul turned to look at the man at the table.

"Do you wish a car or would you like one of my men to drive you?"

"They can drive us back. A car would only be an additional problem for us right now."

"Fine. We shall be in the old bazaar at two. Where do you want us?"

"We will be outside Talmad's Café. . . next to the silversmith in the Street of the Beggars."

"Let me tell my people. . . then we will go." Jacob got up. Abdul looked at him with a frown.

"What do you mean, 'we'?"

"I am your shadow. I and one of my men will be by your side until this is finished, or until someone calls me home. Those are my orders and I am not one to disobey." Jacob raised a hand to stop the protest that he knew was going to come. "It is not debatable. . . it is a given."

Abdul knew when he was beat on a point, so he slumped into a gloomy silence that lingered throughout the journey back to the hotel. Jean Philippe sat in the front seat next to a young Israeli driver and Jacob occupied the back seat with Abdul. The drive ended as it began, in heavy silence.

CHAPTER TWENTY-ONE

"Keep changing your style of doing things."
Baltasar Gracian

After dropping the others at the hotel, the Israeli driver, Avi, parked the car a few blocks away. On the way to the hotel he picked up some fresh rolls and coffee for everyone. Avi sat next to the window eating his breakfast and watching the garden below. Jacob busied himself making notes and planning his movements. Abdul took a shower and changed clothes. He came out in his black robes and wearing heavy framed glasses. Jean Philippe agreed to take one burden off of Abdul and went to the apothecary to pick up the supplies Abdul needed — six empty glass vials in a case, a bottle of glycerin, and some blue food coloring.

When Jean Philippe returned, he smiled at the younger man sitting in the window and thanked him for the sweet roll. He sat on the bed next to the headboard and ate it like a greedy child. The young Israeli handed him a cup of coffee to go with it. Jean Philippe relished it as though it was a rare bottle of fine wine.

"I love the mornings here. They start out warm. I often wonder why I don't move to where I can have breakfast on the terrace every morning." The warmth of the coffee flooded him and he felt the sugar surge through his veins.

"I have a small house by the sea. My wife and I were planning to do that very thing when I retired." Jacob remarked and then returned to his silence and notes.

"Were planning?" Jean Philippe looked at the older man.

"She died a few years ago."

"Pardon. I did not know. Do you still have the place?" Jean Philippe tried to change the conversational direction.

"Yes, but it is not the same. The mornings there are beautiful, though. I can sit and watch the lapping of the waves on the beach and eat fruit from my own trees." Jacob had a sense of suddenly being far away. A flood of memories, both good and bad turned his mind from any other thoughts for a moment.

"Sounds wonderful."

"It would have been." Jacob went back to his notes and Jean Philippe looked at the young man sitting on the window seat. He looked toward the garden and slowly shook his head.

"I think this is yours?" Abdul handed Jacob his wallet with a photograph on top. It was the one of Ann. Jacob took both and looked up at the large man standing over him. He seemed to have changed countenance since donning the robes of the church.

"Yes. . . thank you. I thought I had lost it forever." He lovingly looked at the picture and put it back in the wallet.

Abdul stood there a moment looking down at the man, wondering what inner turmoil drove him. Abdul also had lost someone he loved a long time ago, and knew the pain of loss deep inside. It is something that never goes away; it is just hidden from sight, until those lonely nights come when the wind howls at the corner of the house, and one walks the length of the room a thousand times wondering what could have been different. Abdul gently pushed the thought back into the cerebral darkness where he kept his memories secreted.

Abdul walked over to the dresser and took out the things Jean Philippe had bought for him.

Taking the bottle of glycerin, he poured about a quarters-worth of it down the sink. He then added the blue food coloring to the remainder of the bottle and shook it hard. It took a few moments for the mixture to completely take on a light blue color. Abdul then measured an equal amount into each of the six empty vials. He closed the lids and looked at them for comparison's sake. He then went over and retrieved a candle he had taken from the bar downstairs and lit it. As it burned he dripped the hot wax around the top of the lid of each bottle. He then replaced all of them into the case from which they had come. Abdul then closed the lid of the case and started to wrap the box in foil and brown paper. The other men in the room watched and wondered about his actions.

"What are you doing?" Avi still sitting at the window could no longer contain his curiosity. He was certain that this man had 'gone around the bend'.

"I am making up the package that everyone wants so desperately. You know. . ." he looked at Jacob and smiled, "the one that has the chemical/biological warfare agent in it that is genetically specific to the Israelis."

"Are you telling me that it does not exist. . . or that you no longer have it?" Jacob felt his face flush with anger.

"It never existed. Nobody ever built it, and the only true thing is this!" He held up the wrapped package. "This is the package that the Archbishop and his friends want. . . that you thought you wanted. . . and that everyone that knew about it wanted." He tossed the package to Jean Philippe. "As they said in the old American movie, *this is the stuff that dreams are made of.*"

"Or nightmares." Jacob looked again at the package. "Then Abraham did not have it?"

"He had a package, the same one that I gave him when I set this up. It was supposed to be from the Iraqis, but what the hell, a wrapped package is just that. The old bastard was too scared to look at it, and yet he wanted to so badly. He hoped that it would be used on you and your people, Jacob. Abraham could not wait for it to get to those that wanted it." Abdul took the package back. Jean Philippe gave Abdul a puzzled look. "The package in my safe?"

"I will tell you about that when this is done, but it does not have anything dangerous in it either."

Abdul busied himself with a couple of other items in the room.

"Then from where did our information about this come?" Jacob was unconvinced.

"I planted it where I knew your folks would find it. . . and find it they did." Abdul turned and put the package on the dresser. "Now all I have to do is find a computer and find out if act three is going to get played out today."

***

At nine thirty, Father Leno sat at his computer terminal and watched the last of the details come across his screen. He completed the final transaction and moved all the money out of Switzerland to a bank in the Bahamas. Well not all of it, but all of it that he could find, ninety seven percent of the money. Leno had never handled so much in his career. The priest understood how important this was, so he made three different inquires to make sure that the parts and pieces of the transactions were complete. Leno was given assurance from the supervisor of accounts and the president of the bank's main branch in London that all the monies were accounted for and in place in the new account. Sitting back in his chair he picked up his rosary. For one minute he bowed his head in quiet prayer and then picked up the telephone to call the Pope's private line.

The voice on the other end was that of one of the young priests that worked closely with the Pope. This man had always shown great respect in his dealings with Leno and the Older Man liked him a great deal. He asked for the Pope. Without question there was a pause and then the Holy Father picked up the line.

"Yes, Father Leno?"

"It is done, Your Holiness."

"Until later. . . my thanks and blessings on you, my son."

The line went dead and Leno sat back. He prayed while fingering his rosary and then looked at his desk, realizing that he had to do something about the shortage of Swiss Guards for this weekend's 'high mass' the Pope was organizing. He looked at the schedule on the wall and wondered where he was going to get some bodies to fit into those eccentric uniforms.

***

Abdul found the small cyber-café that Jean Philippe had discovered the day before in his wanderings around the old bazaar. It was amazing to see this small place in the middle of the *Old Quarter's* of one of the oldest cities in the world. He thought for a moment about how the modern world had invaded. The café was a punk-oriented mélange of coffee, computers, navel piercing and tattoos all under one roof and situated in the small alleyway next to a rug merchant on one side and a bakery on the other. Abdul went in and made the arrangements to use one of the terminals. After logging on, he directed the machine to his e-mail account, which was based in Rome. As he waited for his mail to appear on the screen, he turned and watched the passing throng of people visiting the old bazaar. A young girl with pink hair and a ring in her nose walked up to him and started to speak to him in broken English.

"Hey man, I didn't think you guys knew how to use computers?" She sat down next to him and looked him over.

"Some of us are not still in the Dark Ages."

"Wow, man, what a scar you got. Can I touch it?" Without answering she ran her fingers down the side of Abdul's face. Her nails were painted black and she had a silver ring on each finger of her hand. "I got a tattoo." She pulled her blouse partly open to expose the top of her breast where she had a small tattoo of a sunfish. "Isn't it cool, man?"

124

"I got one too." He rolled his sleeve up and showed her the circular Ring and Wing emblem of the 2nd Paratroopers. (When he had left Africa, a few of the boys had gotten him really drunk and he woke up in the morning wearing their brand.)

"Wow. . . Awesome!" She looked up at him. She had far too much makeup on, and she had plucked her eyebrows until there was almost no hair on them at all. Just a thin hint of some color used as an outline for an accent. "You wanna like go and smoke some hash and we can make love all afternoon?"

"Inviting offer. . . but as you can see, I am already spoken for." He indicated his robes.

"All you guys fool around. . . just some of ya are more quiet about it. It will only cost you for the hash." She touched him again on the face. "I like that face and want to see it over me."

"You're a darling, but I need to go and take care of business."

Abdul shut down the computer and went over to the kid at the desk, a dark-eyed youth who was taking exception to the actions of the younger girl and this older priest. Abdul asked what he owed and paid him. The young man glared at Abdul, who was going to let it go by but then thought better of it. He turned back and leaned across the counter so he could speak quietly to the youth. "Keep it in your pants, 'stick'. . . unless you want it ripped off and fed to you."

The young Turk flared and pointed at the door, "Get out. . . Get out and don't come back!"

"Don't plan to unless it is to dance with you." He winked and walked out. The young girl was cozying up to some other customer now. Abdul walked down the avenue and turned on another alley, all the time aware of Jacob and the young Israeli, Avi following him twenty paces to his rear. Abdul stopped and opened the piece of paper the girl with the pink hair had slipped into his hand. He opened it and read it slowly. He tossed it on the ground as he laughed and walked on. When Jacob got to the spot that Abdul had stopped, he picked up the crumpled piece of paper and read: "You are being followed; you must lose them before we can meet."

Jacob put it inside his coat pocket and continued to follow him up the street back toward the hotel.

When they went into the hotel, Jacob took the stairs and left the young man to watch the foyer for any activities. Once on the third floor he went into Abdul's room and handed him back the note. "What is this all about? I thought you weren't working with anyone except, Jean Philippe?" Jacob tossed his coat on the chair, bristling with anger and frustration. He rubbed his hands and walked to the window.

"All the note proves is that we are being watched also. They already have the bazaar staked out and are waiting for the prime players to appear." Abdul laughed again. He looked at Jean Philippe and showed with a gesture of his hand that he could not talk right now. "Better get a hold of your folks and have them go straight to the bazaar and start looking around to see if they can pick up on how many of these people are out there. This just keeps getting better and better."

"Who was the girl?" Jacob was not amused.

"Someone obviously paid to give me the note. They thought it was better than showing themselves. Last time a couple of them did so, I understand they ended up dead. So I think they are going to be a little standoffish. Wouldn't you say?" Abdul turned and again looked at Jacob. Something had changed. Jacob looked at Abdul the way a huntsman watches a fox.

"What do you know that we don't?" Jacob looked hard at Abdul.

"A secret." Abdul walked into the washroom.

***

"My mother told me stories when I was a child, that if I was not always good, one of the devil's underlings would come for me and drag me into the pit of hell from where I could never escape. She frightened me into being a good boy and vigorously studying my music. At night I would fear that the door of the small closet at the end of the bed would open and out would come a drooling, red-eyed demon to grab me. I would fight but lose and he would drag me under the house to where I knew hell was only meters away, waiting for me. I would cry myself to sleep. I would awaken to find Papa there, sitting next to my bed. I would tell him my fear and he would tell me not to believe in demons. He said there was nothing to fear." Jean Philippe talked as they walked into the bazaar. Abdul was in his robes and Jean Philippe wore the collar of a monk. "But you know something? I still fear closed doors on closets. I still either leave them open or take the doors off completely.

"Does this story have a point?" Abdul smiled at his friend.

"No. It is just filler. I want to know what happened when you left the hotel. . . that made all of this shit make sense to you, and I can't ask." Jean Philippe motioned toward another side street.

"It is a done deal. This. . . what we are about to do is just window dressing. All we have to do right now is not get ourselves killed."

"Simple. Same as always, isn't it? Only this time we have one group who wants to shoot us on sight, and the other ones who are here to protect us are less than charmed by your style. It is wonderful being here with you. It is like being on a holiday." He looked up the side streets and watched every doorway.

"Ninety minutes, my friend, and we should be through with all of this. There will only be the shouting and screaming from the sidelines." Abdul was full of himself, that was clear to Jean Philippe.

"But what if it gets dicey?"

"Well, then we are going to break and run like spot-tailed gazelles and head for the hills. There is no reason to be a hero today, not now." Abdul pointed at the small café and they headed toward it. They had not seen any of Jacob's people, but they felt their presence all around, moving and relocating as they moved through the streets.

CHAPTER TWENTY-TWO

"Be not afraid on any man, no matter what his size;
when in need call on me, and I shall equalize."
Side plate quote on the Colt Peacemaker Pistol. 1868

The afternoon heat hung in the old bazaar. The scent of saffron, spices, human sweat, and incense filled the air. As old as history itself, the sounds of ancient occupations assailed the ears, and people of all colors passed by the old café where the two men dressed in Roman blacks sat and drank their coffee. It was ten past three in the afternoon. Jean Philippe had looked at his watch every minute for the past six minutes then he would look up and down the street. Somewhere in the throng of faces, men he knew and men he did not know waited for each other. He realized that there now were enough guns in this small part of town to start a small war. Here with his friend he sat playing at man's second oldest profession. It was not like the nights in the bush where one had some kind of idea who your enemy was. Here, the enemy could be anyone. There are no rules, he knew that, but this was foolish to sit here in the open waiting for an unknown danger to walk up and say 'hello'.

"I know." Abdul turned and looked at him. He had said volumes in that one phrase, but yet it did not ease the tension.

"If they don't show, then what?" Jean Philippe put down his cup. "I don't think your new friends are going to like that very much."

"My new friends? I think they have not yet adjusted to the idea that twenty four hours ago they were ready to kill me, and now they want us to take them home and introduce them to the family." Abdul pushed his coffee cup away and lit another cigarette.

"Not enough room in my place for them. They would break some-thing - they are very clumsy." Jean Philippe smiled at his little joke, re-membering the accident in his shop back in Paris.

"I hope not." Abdul tightened.

Jean Philippe let his hand go limp in his lap.

"Father Lindquist. . . Brother Baptiste. . . how are my faithful ser-vants doing?" Archbishop Giovanni's English was broken, but passable.

"Still serving our True Master." Abdul did not look up. The man stood there and then finally sat down.

"Your True Master? Oh, money or whores. I forget what a Judas like you works for these days." Giovanni's hatred showed in his eyes. "You have something that is mine."

"You don't want this." Abdul pulled the package from his belt and placed it on the table between Jean Philippe and himself. "It could mean the end to everything you care about."

"You stupid imbecile! Did you think that someone like you can stand in the way of what I have spent my life building? You're more ignorant than most of these dumb bastards walking through this flea-infested back of beyond."

"It never ceases to amaze me how, as men become more holy, their language begins to sound more like that of angels." Abdul looked straight at the man. His hard eyes bored into Giovanni, who represented everything that Abdul hated in life, hypocrisy incarnate. Angels from the dark side of Heaven were amateurs in comparison to Giovanni.

"Let's get this done. I have better things to do than spending my day in idle talk with two losers like you. My God, you are a disgrace to the vestments you wear." Giovanni motioned to someone to come over. A middle-aged man in civilian clothing walked up next to the Archbishop and stood.

"Let me have my package." Giovanni reached out, but Abdul slapped his hand away. The other man started to reach inside his jacket, when Giovanni held up his hand to stop the action. "Not here and not now, but when we are done, you had better run and find the deepest and darkest hole in which to hide. There will be people looking for you. You know that, don't you?" Giovanni remarked while rubbing the back of his hand.

"Have you transferred my money?" Abdul held onto the package.

"Of course, it was there yesterday. If you had checked you would have known."

"I did and it was. But I just wanted to hear you tell me that you had transferred it, Archbishop." Abdul got up and Jean Philippe followed. He tossed the package to the Swiss Guard standing next to the Archbishop. "There it is, have fun." He started to walk away.

"Wait a minute! You expect me to take your word on it, that this is the stuff we have been waiting for?" Two or three men moved out of the crowd and formed a line to block off his exit.

"Open the box!" Abdul leaned very close. "But remember if any of the seals are broken on even one bottle, it will probably kill ten thousand people in four square miles from here. . . including you."

Giovanni took the box and unwrapped it. He took out one of the bottles and peered into it.

"It only kills Jews?" Giovanni sneered.

"True, in the form of vapor. When disbursed via an airborne vector, it will have the effect you want. However, in liquid form like this, it does not discriminate as to whom it kills. Victims normally die in fifteen to twenty minutes, bleeding from every orifice and strangling on their own blood and body fluids." Abdul touched the bottle lightly. "In your hands you are holding the worst form of death imaginable. I hope you did not get any on yourself, Your Eminence."

Giovanni pushed the bottle down into the box and handed it back to the Guard. "You had better not try to screw with me, Lindquist. I have a long reach and people who know how to cause a great deal of pain."

"Good connections for a priest. Good day Archbishop." Abdul and Jean Philippe turned and started to walk away. The men blocking the way were not moving.

"Let them go. I will deal with them later." Giovanni got up and started in the other direction.

Under his coat Jean Philippe was holding onto the grip of his gun while watching the men mill around behind him. "That's it?"

"Far from it. But let us just walk away, old friend, and let others deal with picking up the pieces."

Abdul and his friend wove through the crowd and disappeared, followed by a few of their new friends.

CHAPTER TWENTY-THREE

"The moving finger writes and having writ moves on,
Nor all of your piety or wit can lure it back to cancel out a half a line
Nor all your tears wash out one word of it."
The Rubaiyat - Omar Khayyam

Abdul and Jean Philippe moved quickly through the crowd of people in the bazaar, weaving down back alleys and side streets. The perspiration was rolling down Abdul's back and he knew something was not right. An old instinct, or perhaps a habit, overcame him. He pushed Jean Philippe into a doorway just as a bullet struck above his head. Ancient mortar and plaster exploded as the high speed round slammed into the wall.

"What the hell is this all about?!" Jean Philippe had his pistol out and was now kneeling in the darkness and gloom of a room into which they had just burst into.

"Payback. You really didn't think that Giovanni was going to let us just walk out of this city alive, did you?" Abdul was stripping off his robe and underneath he wore a pair of black jeans and a black tee shirt. "I know too much. I double-crossed him and that cost him another five million U. S. dollars, out of his special account. I know what the package has in it and I know what he plans to do with it. He is just pissed off enough, that on nothing more than general principal, he wants to kill me. You are just an extra bit of pleasure for him."

"Wonderful. Where the hell are your new friends?" Jean Philippe pulled back from the doorway just enough to be missed by the next fusillade of 9mm rounds that smashed into the doorframe. "I thought they weren't supposed to leave your side. So much for promises, oui?"

"They are out there, but this is tricky as hell for them, too. They commit too quickly and they have got a lot of explaining to do in an Arab country." He looked around the room to see if it offered another way out. "Besides, nobody really wants a bunch of dead guys laying around the streets. . . it isn't good for business."

"Just us. That would be okay with everyone, I think." Jean Philippe ripped his jacket and collar off.

"I can't even see the son of a bitch that is shooting at us. Can you?"

"No. He is on the roof. That is the only thing that saved us. He didn't compensate for firing at a downward angle. But I figure the shooter has learned from that mistake and right about now he won't miss, if we give him a chance." Abdul jogged across the room to the window on the other side. The hissing sound of a silencer filled the air as four bullets tore through the wooden slats of the shutter. Debris scattered all over the room. Abdul jumped back and crashed into the wall. He was narrowly missed by all but one of the bullets. He looked down and saw the small rivulet of blood running down his arm; the bullet had grazed him, ripping flesh and muscle, but had done no major damage.

"You're hit!" Jean Philippe had his back to wall as another blast of shells rained into the gloom of the room.

"Don't worry, it's just a scratch. These guys are firing for effect and hoping to hit something. They aren't professionals, old friend." Abdul crouched in the corner.

"Great, that does not mean they are not going to get lucky and still kill us." Jean Philippe dodged to the other side of the doorframe trying to get a fix on the shooter on the roof.

"Well there is always that possibility, but I am not of a mind to let them get lucky today. In fact, these little bastards have just pissed me off enough to show them what war really looks like." Abdul could feel the adrenalin pumping through his bloodstream.

"Oh no, don't get mad." Jean Philippe moved to the doorframe and jumped back quickly just as another round hit the floor and threw up wood shavings into his face.

"Let's provide an introduction to Purgatory!" Abdul wrapped his hand around the old oil lamp that sat on the table and broke off the chimney. He turned the wick up an inch and a half, then lit the lamp with his cigarette lighter and yelled to Jean Philippe, "Covering fire!"

Jean Philippe dropped to one knee and opened up, spraying the rooftop of the building across the alley with heavy slugs. At the same moment, Abdul hurled the lamp right at the corner of the roof. It exploded throwing burning kerosene in the direction of the hidden shooter. There was a yell as the improvised explosive did its job, raining burning kerosene into the face of the shooter on the roof. He made his final error when he jumped up to snuff out the flaming cinders in his face with his hands. Abdul fired one shot that struck the man between his two hands and drove a bullet directly into his brain. He fell forward over the parapet and crashed into the street, his face still burning with kerosene. The moment that he hit the ground, Jean Philippe hurled himself at a right angle out the door and let go with three quick shots that struck the other gunman in the groin and stomach. His machine pistol with silencer flew from his hands as he grabbed at the spurting blood and intestines that fell onto his shoes. He doubled over and groaned as life drained out of him.

"Now!" Jean Philippe was back against the wall waving to Abdul to move past him, which the other man did. Abdul made it to the corner and scanned both ways. He waved to Jean Philippe to advance. The next movements were like a well-choreographed dance. The two men moved from wall to wall, checking doorways, roofs, and any other dark places where someone might be hiding. The shots and the explosions had alerted the people who lived in the area to get inside and stay down. As Abdul looked back, he could see smoke rising from the building he had firebombed. In the distance he could hear the sound of police and fire companies rushing to the area.

"We need to get out of here!" Abdul looked over to Jean Philippe who was picking wood splitters out of his face.

"I agree we should get out of here, but you tell me which way you would like to go? Back into the center of the bazaar would be suicide at this point and a lot of innocent people would get hurt. These guys are not good, but there are a bunch of them, and they want to kill us."

"Yeah, but this is nothing but dead ends and rabbit warrens in here. Hell, I have no idea which way is even out. If we stay too long, I am sure that the locals will start telling police where we are and that only increases our odds of getting dead."

"Is it time to pray?" Jean Philippe smiled his sarcastic smirk.

"I already have and my soul is ready to meet its creator." Abdul turned the corner and used his gun as a pointing instrument, sweeping it in a half circle ready to fire at any movement he perceived. "It is just my body that still longs for the flesh pits of the world and the sordid life which I have grown to enjoy."

"You had no Creator or Maker. You were glued together from parts taken from dead paratroopers and given life by some whore in Corsica who walked on your chest with high heels until you started to breathe; and with that, you went on to cause all your friends nothing but problems." Jean Philippe moved around Abdul and checked the alleyway.

"You're my only friend."

"That is exactly what I mean." Jean Philippe jerked back at the next corner just as two men opened fire with small automatic machine pistols, filling the air with fifteen to twenty bullets that sounded like angry bees whizzing by. "Damn!"

"You okay?" Abdul moved close and checked his weapon's magazine for ammunition.

"No, my pride is hurt beyond belief. Who in the hell do these guys think they are? I am Jean Philippe Emanuel Baptiste, Officer of the Legion, winner of the Legion of Honor and right now, one damn mad Frenchman." He jumped and rolled across the ground. This caught the other two gunmen off-guard and their shots were high. Jean Philippe's were not. Four bullets were fired from his MAB 9mm pistol and four bullets ripped into the bodies of two young Swiss Guards who had never before been in combat. The impact threw them both backwards into boxes of garbage. Jean Philippe was over them in a second, picking up their weapons and additional clips. He stood and looked down at them, "Who the hell did you think you were shooting at, scum?" He spat on one of them and ran back to where Abdul was guarding the rear of the action.

"That was really brave and about the stupidest thing I have ever seen done." Abdul took one of the weapons and pushed his own handgun into his belt.

"Yeah, well they have really started to piss me off. These shooters who this Bishop of yours sent are children and amateurs." Jean Philippe stood up and looked around. "And where the hell is the great Israeli army that was here to protect our butts?!"

"Calm down, big fellow. We still have a ways to go." Abdul looked around the corner.

"Bull shit, that is what this is!" Jean Philippe stood up and started to walk down the middle of the street.

"J. P., what the hell are you doing?" Abdul moved along the wall, covering the big man.

"Getting them to show themselves, the little pigs." Jean Philippe walked into the crossroads of the two alleys and looked both ways.

"You're going to get yourself killed!" Abdul was beside himself.

"Not likely. These guys are pack-feeders. They need each other to get their courage up. We have taken out four of them," he jerked his thumb toward the two men he had left dead in the alley, "and the others know it. They have radios on so they know that these two and the two we killed up there are gone. That won't give them a lot of courage to come out in a straight up fight, so they are going to try to take us from ambush. That is the way these little 'sons of a bitches' think."

"Wonderful, a tactical lecture in the middle of a firefight. You bucking for a job at the War College in Paris?" Abdul had pulled him to the wall and got the big man down.

"I would like to teach school like you, but what the hell, this is what I am good at." Jean Philippe in a single movement arched the machine pistol through the air and fired a continuous blast at the opposite roof line. Unprepared, Abdul wrenched away from the muzzle blast that was next to his head. A scream filled the air and a body crashed down less than two meters away from the men. Another of the Swiss Guards had died in the backstreets of Istanbul.

"This is not going the way anybody thought it would happen. . . especially me. I was sure Giovanni would wait until they could get me on flat killing grounds and make it clean and with no witnesses. This is just crazy!" Abdul felt his arm where the bullet had grazed him and found that the bleeding had stopped.

"Giovanni is more desperate than you know, but something is wrong with all of this. Where are the Israelis?" A bullet hit directly next to Abdul's head. Flying plaster peppered the side of his face and he felt blood spatters hit his face. The bullet had broken apart and a piece of it had hit Jean Philippe in the side of the face, just in front of his jawbone and it had torn a gash in his cheek. Abdul knew that the wound was not life-threatening, but the shooters were trying to be. Abdul and Jean Philippe hit the ground in opposite directions bringing their guns to bear on the new shooter in the blue sports jacket. But suddenly the man fell forward, with a large hole drilled into his back. Standing behind the fallen man was the young Israeli, Avi; their driver from the night before. He ran up to Abdul and Jean Philippe to help them to their feet. Then he pushed them up against the wall and formed a shield in front of them with his own body.

"Where the hell have you been? Those pricks have been trying to kill us!" Jean Philippe looked down at the dark Semitic man.

"All perdition broke loose up there when you two made that first turn. Before we could get beyond you, we had those assholes all over us. We got four or five of them, wounded a couple of others, and in the fight, Jacob caught one." He pulled a small two-way radio from his pocket and spoke into it rapidly in Hebrew.

"Is he okay? Jacob, is he alright?" Abdul showed true concern.

"Yeah. It is minor, but he bleeds like a goat with its throat cut. I got Jacob out with two others back to the safe-house, and now I'm here to get you two out without being stopped by the police." He was listening to the radio.

"It's alright. . . we're alright. . . calm down." Abdul looked over at Jean Philippe whom had returned to his normal, dry, and gloomy expression.

"Maybe you're alright, but I'm wounded." Jean Philippe touched his face.

"You cut yourself worse when you shave with that antique you call a razor."

"It was my father's and it is made of good Damascus steel, I will have you know."

The young Israeli looked at them as though he had walked into a different world.

"Don't worry, we will get you out of here." Jean Philippe said to the young man who was showing signs of fatigue.

"I am suppose to get 'YOU' out of here!"

"Oh." Jean Philippe smiled. "If that is the case, then proceed."

"I don't give a good God damn who gets whom out. . . but I am making tracks right now!" Abdul started to look down the alley through which he planned to leave.

"Wait just a minute. . . Isam will be here with the car."

"Isam, do I know him? I don't ride with anyone I don't know. My mother made me promise never to get into a car with strangers. I have always kept that promise to my mother. Who is Isam?" Jean Philippe was looking down at Avi who was at least six inches shorter.

"He is one of us! You saw him last night!" Avi was looking around almost in a panic and not believing he was having this conversation.

"That means we don't have to walk? Good. Then I will go with Isam." Jean Philippe smiled.

"It better be quick, 'cause I am not really interested in shooting police today, and there is no way I am going to spend a night in a Turkish jail." Abdul was watching every angle that he could and did not see any movement.

"I saw that movie," Jean Philippe looked at Abdul. "I liked the girl with the great body that hid the hundred dollar bills in the book-cover."

"Now, here he is. Down this way and into the car!" The young Israeli moved out quickly and dashed in front of the other two men. The car sped around one corner and all of them were in it and gone in less than thirty seconds. Abdul sat back and rubbed the side of his face and then put a battle compress on his arm wound. Jean Philippe put a cloth next to the cut on his cheek and closed his eyes. The ride back to the safe-house was uneventful.

***

As Giovanni's car was speeding back to the airport, Fathers' Marcus and Anthony sat in the jump-seats of the limo listening to him carefully. The two priests were aware that his disposition was a little shakier than either of them had seen before. This arrogant man had today played at a game and had mainly lost. This did not go down well with Giovanni and he was taking it out on the closest objects to him, his two assistants.

"Those bastards! Who do they think they are screwing with?" Giovanni exploded again for the third time in as many miles. Father Marcus turned away and closed his eyes. He had never believed that he would work for an Archbishop who sounded like a common dockside sailor. He was in too deep, he knew it. Giovanni knew too much about his private life and Marcus was never going to give up the chance to replace this man as head of OSC. He was use to the intrigue of church politics, but would have never thought that he would see the *men of the cloth* fighting in the streets with guns and claiming that it was for the 'church's' good.

His thoughts were interrupted by Giovanni's voice again. "When we get back to Rome, you put out a communiqué that someone tried to assassinate me. Make it look like the Israelis, but don't use that term. The Swiss Guards died protecting me. Round up those who are left alive, the bumbling idiots and isolate them somewhere until I can figure out what to do with them. I should have used our own people. The "Gruppen Siben" would have gotten the job done. That is for sure." He lit a large cigar and puffed away, filling the car with noxious vapors. The younger priest was turning green from the smoke. "You, Father Anthony, you need to take this to Brazen in Florence and have him run the laboratory check on it to make sure that it is as lethal as promised." He handed the package to the younger man, who was reluctant to touch it.

"Come on take it, it won't bite you. What is wrong? You scared you might have enough Jew blood in you to be harmed?" Giovanni pushed the package into the other mans hands.

The younger priest looked at Giovanni with a flat cold stare. "First, I have no Jewish blood in me. "Second, I am not scared of you or anything else. Third, that cluster you created today in the old bazaar was the single most idiotic gesture I have ever witnessed. And finally, remember whom you serve. It would not be hard to have you replaced at any point in time. There are those that think you have outlasted your usefulness at present. Don't anger me to the point of joining that view."

Then Father Anthony took the package and sat it in his lap, turning and looking out the window.

"We need to move the time schedule up. Once you get back from Brazen's we will start Phase Two. Still we need to get rid of those two piss ants, Lindquist and Baptiste. Marcus, get a hold of Rodin in Rome and tell him we want to put a contract out on those two 'sons of bitches'."

Marcus did not acknowledge his superior.

"Father Marcus, I gave you an order. Did you not hear it?"

"I heard it. But, my God, how far does this go? We are now hiring killers to remove people because they threaten us?"

"You weak simpleton. How did I ever think I could trust you to assist me in this effort? Of course we kill people. What do you think this is about?" He grabbed the package from the younger priest and pushed it into the other man's face. "We are getting ready to commit genocide on a whole group of people and you are squeamish about killing two ex-priests?"

"That is different. Those are Jews we are planning to exterminate. They are not like us. Lindquist and Baptiste are our own people." Marcus retorted, showing a hint of his bigotry as well as some hidden knowledge.

"What is the difference? Anything that stands in the way of our plans needs to be corrected. Today was a minor upset, but it does not change anything, gentlemen. We are going to protect our assets and make a difference in the process. Remember that!" Giovanni sat back, disgusted with the man. He was already thinking of how he would replace Marcus. He knew that he needed more help anyway, but to select and train new members into the Special Office took time. He would have to turn them slowly and check and recheck their loyalty to him and not to the church. It took too much time, but that is the way that he had learned. And that is the method he knew that he must continue to use, until the time he controlled the whole Vatican. Then things would operate a little different. Giovanni looked over at Father Anthony. He was Giovanni's greatest danger. One telephone call from him and Giovanni knew that someone would show up and there would be an opening for a new Archbishop. He needed to complete this task successfully. Then Father Anthony and his friends would help him obtain the position on the 'Chair of Peter' as Pope. Failure was not an option at this point, for the consequences would be too great. Giovanni realized that he was just one more puppet that a large powerful and secret organization used to accomplish its goals. Once he became Pope he then could turn the tide on them and eventually he believed he could control them.

***

The Pope read the dispatch again carefully. He held his chest and felt his heart beat. He got up and walked to the window and looked down on St. Peter's Square. He did not believe it. When it started he thought those who had brought him the information must be jealous and spiteful. But as time had gone by, he had learned more and more of the truth, and it had sickened him. The Pope looked at the towers of the church across the square and wondered if he would live long enough to correct this thing. He has never admitted to himself that he was capable of such deep hatred but for the first time in his eighty-two years of life he felt its cold hand embrace him. He pushed the thought away and stood there. The knock on the door was almost unheard in his present state of mind. The young priest that attends him opened it and ushered Father Leno into the room and indicated that he should sit. Leno did, and waited without comment for the Pope to acknowledge him.

"Father, how long have you served me here?" The Pope did not turn around.

"Since you came, Your Holiness."

"And before, how long were you here at the Vatican?"

"Five years."

"You are one of the few people who I trust. Did you know that, Giuseppe?" Leno had never been addressed by his Christian name by any of the Cardinals or the Pope in all the time he had been at the Vatican. He was taken back for a moment.

"You place too much trust in this old man, Your Holiness. I am just a servant." Leno hung his head in humility.

"You are much more than that. Father Leno. I must do things in the next few days that should never be asked of a religious man. I must become involved in secular actions that will affect millions of people's lives. I am going to commit actions that I know I will answer to God for later. But in all of that, I must do what my conscience dictates, and I need your help." The Pope turned and walked over to where the other man was sitting and laid a hand on his shoulder, indicating that he should remain seated.

"Whatever the Holy Father needs of this poor priest, all he must do is tell him, and I shall comply."

"Don't be too quick to offer, Father. This is a great and terrible task I lay at your feet." The Pope sat down and again looked at the communiqué.

"If it is for Your Holiness and the church, I will do it, or die trying." The man glowed with stubbornness.

The Pope nodded his approval of the man's willingness to serve. "Three things, all great and beyond the understanding of a simple man like yourself, but necessary to complete." He grew silent for a moment considering the right wording. "First, when Archbishop Giovanni and his staff land at the airport this evening, I want all of them placed under house-arrest and guarded. They are to talk to or see no one, until I say so."

Leno was shocked. He was visibly shaken to the core of his being. He knew that Giovanni controlled more Cardinals and Bishops than anyone and this order was going to have great repercussions in every corner of the Vatican. He looked at the man across from him. A hundred different questions all starting with the word 'why' ran through his mind. "Yes, Your Excellency. I will handle it personally."

"Second, send all the Swiss Guards home. Tell the coordinator in Zurich that their loyalty has been compromised and I personally want a new battalion here within the month. Until then, hire whoever you think can protect our facility. Get someone who you can trust. Ask the Rome Police for help or the army. I just want to make sure this establishment is protected against all enemies right now." The Pope looked down again at the paper in front of him.

"It shall be done." Leno knew exactly who he was going to call. He had been given the instructions via the Internet even before the Pope had ordered it done.

"Thirdly, and most importantly right now." He hesitated, looking deep inside for the right words.

"You told me you have family and friends that can do things?" The emphasis was on the word *things*." Leno heard it clearly.

"Yes Holiness."

"We have two priests that are being assisted by the Israeli intelligence service in Istanbul who I need to have here by Friday; alive." He turned to the man and looked directly at him. "Father, if there is any chance you cannot do this, tell me now, for I need in my soul to know that these two men's lives will be spared and that they will be standing in front of me on Friday."

"Sir with all due respect, if you want them here on Friday, I shall promise on my immortal soul, it will be done."

The Pope handed Leno the file. It contained all the information on Abdul, Jean Philippe, and the contacts with the Israelis. "I also need this man brought here." The Pope pointed to one of the names on the list. "Unharmed and no one is to be injured. . . but this needs to be done."

Without a word Father Leno stood and bowed, then walked from the Papal Office down the staircase and back to his office. He did not want to be involved in any of this. He had joined the church to avoid following the criminal path of his father and older brothers in Sicily, but now he knew that to protect that thing that he loved most, the Church and his Pope, he needed his family and their contacts with those known as the 'Mafia'.

CHAPTER TWENTY-FOUR

"If you do not go to war, He will punish you sternly, and will replace you by other men. You will in no way harm Him, for God has power over all things."
Holy Koran - Book of Repentance

Abdul finished sewing up Jean Philippe's cheek with supplies taken from the medical kit that the Israelis carried with them on all missions. He had cleaned his own wound and put a field dressing on it. Some of the other men had helped Jacob with his leg wound and Abdul walked in to see how the older man was doing. Jacob had his leg resting on a pillow on the stool in front of his chair.

"How is it with the leg?" Abdul looked at the dressing which appeared to be an expert job.

"I don't think I will be playing soccer for the Israeli Olympic Team this year." Jacob winced in pain.

"Do you want something for the pain?"

"Yes, but I won't take anything because someone here has to keep his wits about them. I don't think I can trust you two to stay calm and collected." Jacob made a little jibe at the actions that had been taken earlier in the afternoon in the bazaar.

"We got through it."

"Yes, but the cost was high and I fear that this will not be the end of it. We still need to get you both out of here and back to Israel." Jacob moved in his chair trying to find that one spot where nothing would hurt.

Abdul off-handedly remarked. "We're not heading in that direction, but I need to get to Rome. I believe that is what your government wants also." Abdul sat down and adjusted the pillow to give Jacob better support.

"I don't know about that. I know that I was told to keep you alive and the only place that I know of right now where I can do that best is in my country. Going to Rome would put you and your friend right back on the firing line. I don't think that is such a good idea." He noticed the improvement in his resting position. "Thank you, that feels better."

"Good. Well one thing is for sure. We've got to get out of here right away because the Turkish authorities are going to be mighty upset with whomever is responsible for that little affair uptown today and they will be turning over every garbage can and manhole cover to find out who did it."

Abdul walked over and got the pack of cigarettes off the counter and came back and handed them to Jacob, who nodded his appreciation.

"True. We are working on getting all of us south to one of the coastal towns and be picked up. It will be slower, but safer I believe." Jacob pulled an old ordnance map from his haversack and pointed to the area so Abdul could see.

Jean Philippe walked into the room holding Abdul's cell phone. He was talking to someone on it, and handed it not to Abdul, but to Jacob. The older man looked at him and took the phone. Jean Philippe looked at him and said, "It is your boss, I called him." Jacob's mouth fell open.

Abdul turned and looked at Jean Philippe, "Are you going to tell me how you knew who 'his' boss is and how to get a hold of him?"

"A friend in Rome gave me the number." Jean Philippe gave up nothing in his expression.

"Secrets between us?"

"Of course. You have yours and I have mine. The call I made before from the café in the old bazaar, when you wanted to know? I have a few friends left, besides you." He smiled and walked out of the room.

Hiram was speaking slowly and concisely to explain the situation. All hell had broken loose at the Knesset and there was no way that an allocation could be made to rescue them. They had to get out of Turkey on their own. Jacob nodded and covered his face with one of his hands. Some arrangements were being made to assist them from another group, but Hiram did not have the details. He told Jacob that someone would be contacting Jean Philippe with information in the next few hours.

"What are we to do?"

"Let the Frenchman have the lead. Get the team out, and let Abdul and Baptiste go and do whatever they feel is necessary. Just make sure you are with them."

"I don't understand, Hiram?" Jacob was beside himself.

"I know, but this thing is now bigger than us or the country. It has taken on a life of its own and we are being swept along with it. Just keep healthy."

"Easier said than done, but thank you." He closed the phone and handed it back to Abdul.

"So?" Abdul sat there looking at the older man.

"It seems like I am at this point in your hands." Jacob motioned to the other room. "Our French brother will tell us the next step I am told."

"I don't understand any of this." Abdul got up and walked over to the counter and poured a cup of coffee. He stood with his back to the counter looking at the room and the wounded man.

"Who the hell is playing us?"

"Good question." Jacob pulled his notebook out and started to write down events so that he could later write his report.

***

Father Leno was standing at the gate in the private terminal at Rome's airport when the four men came out. They had shown their diplomatic passport to the Customs Officer who waved them through without a second glance. Giovanni was already on his cell phone when Leno walked up and took it away.

"What is this?" Giovanni stared at the small hard man who handed the phone to a man in a black suit behind him.

"You are under house arrest by the order of His Holiness. All of you will come with me without question." Leno gestured for two other men to take the briefcase away from Father Anthony.

"You can't. . ."

"I'm not. It is His Holiness who is doing this. These men are to protect you or if you think that you wish to put up a fight, they are ready to do you great harm. The choice is yours, Excellency." Leno motioned toward a side door and a waiting auto.

"I will not go with you. I am an Archbishop. . ."

He was cut off by a thin man in a dark suit with a pencil thin moustache and flat hard eyes. "You make another sound, I will personally rip your lungs out, so move!"

Leno made a hand signal for the man to back off a little. "My friends are not used to dealing with people of such, how shall I say it. . . quality.

So they may seem a little coarse to you. But then again, I would not push him too far because he will rip your lungs out, Archbishop. Now move, please."

Without further disturbance they climbed into the three waiting vehicles and sped away into the night toward the heart of Rome.

***

The two dark figures moved from the relative safety of the adjoining houses to the open grounds that stretched in front of the safe-house. Each man wore a black outfit so as to blend into the night. They moved slowly and cautiously toward the building.

In a hushed tone one of the men spoke to the other. "Who are these guys?"

"Two of them are some kind of outlaw priests and there's a bunch of Yid gunman. That is all I know, but we've got to make sure they are alive, well and out of Turkey before morning."

"Why?"

"Because somebody called who pays us. . . you oaf. . . and I said so. Somebody is paying us a briefcase full of money to make sure this is done right." The other man was looking through his night-vision glasses at the safe-house in Istanbul.

"They're going to put up a fight?"

"Wouldn't you or me? What do you think? That is why we got to do this quietly." The other man picked up his cell phone and called a number. He spoke briefly and went back to observing the house.

"What are we waiting for?"

"For a sign from God. What do you think?" He turned and looked around at the darkened houses that occupied the area. "We're waiting for a call to tell us that we can come in. I, myself am not interested in bursting into a house with a bunch of guys who have guns and know how to use them." The cell phone rang.

"Okay, let's go. You have everything and know what to say if questioned." The other man patted his chest under his coat.

"Do you think we will need these?"

"You never know." The first man got up and started to walk toward the safe-house followed by the other. Both men wore suits and carried small leather bags. The first man turned on his flashlight and motioned to the truck to move into the driveway to shine the headlights on the windows of the house.

***

Inside the house a young Israeli stuck his head into the room where Jacob was resting.

"We've got company!"

"Get ready. Tell the others, but no shooting unless necessary." Jacob reached down under his hip and pulled his automatic from where he had it hidden in the chair. Abdul was asleep sitting at the kitchen table with his head resting on his arms. Suddenly he became instantly alert.

"What is it?"

"People outside. Probably Turkish Police or Intelligence."

Abdul pulled his weapon and checked the action. He moved to the window then looked out without being seen. "Two." Abdul nodded toward the rear of the house.

"Easy. . . no guns." Jean Philippe was walking through the kitchen.

"What?" Abdul turned to him.

"They are here to help." Jean Philippe opened the door and walked out and greeted the men.

"What is going on?" Abdul stood near the big Frenchman and watched the exchange of greetings with the two strangers.

"They're smugglers. They are going to get us into Greece tonight by boat. A plane will be waiting to take us to Rome." The men indicated that they should leave at once. "It appears the police are on their way here and it is advisable to leave right now."

Abdul turned and walked back inside to tell Jacob and his men to leave everything they could not carry and get outside. Jacob was reluctant to move but when Abdul spoke in Hebrew to the men and explained in a way that only soldiers understood, they picked the older man up and carried him down the hill to the waiting truck. Everyone piled into the back and pulled the curtain to provide concealment. As the driver turned the corner and started down the hill the safe-house erupted in a fireball of an explosion.

"I guess these guys like to cover their tracks." Abdul looked at the fire that spread quickly throughout the old house.

"Hope you didn't leave your favorite keepsake behind?" Jean Philippe nodded at the two cars with blue flashing lights that passed them going up the hill.

"I sure miss the old homestead. You know that?" Abdul grinned.

"This just keeps getting better and better." Jean Philippe sat down and pulled out a pack of cigarettes. Without a question the two men who had come for them each reached over to take two cigarettes and then nodded their thanks.

"You're welcome. . . I think?" Jean Philippe threw the empty pack on the floorboard.

CHAPTER TWENTY-FIVE

"For in much wisdom is much grief: and
he that increaseth knowledge increaseth sorrow."
Ecclesiastes 1:18

At 9:00 P. M. the Pope told his secretary he was accepting no more phones calls from anyone with the exception of the two names that were on the list he handed to the man. His office had been besieged with outside calls and request from Cardinals who needed to be seen at once. Rome was a small town in many ways and the word had spread quickly about the incident at the airport. Factions were already lining up and demands were being made, in polite ways, but the Pope held his ground. He would not grant an audience to any of Giovanni's protectors within the College of Cardinals. He knew that many people, some of them priests were compromised and just plain greedy and that they would come to the Archbishop's aid. These men knew the repercussions that this airport arrest would have far away from the Vatican.

The Pope had heard the rumors that one of the Pope's preceding him had been killed on the orders from Mussolini before the outbreak of World War II. The dictator learned that the Pope would not provide him with support and Papal blessings for his ruthless actions. Politics and religion had always blurred when it came to the power of the Vatican. The Vicar of Rome has great influence over the opinions and beliefs that the people held. If he did not finish this now, he knew that his life would become even shorter than the remaining years he felt he had left. The walls of this ancient palace would not protect him. Only the truth brought into the open would ensure that he could continue to provide the services that he believed his church needed. He had sat and read the document on his desk from cover to cover and he knew what actions needed to be taken in two days. But he needed all of the players on his chessboard to be in place. He closed the file and closed his eyes and prayed.

Guidance seemed to be the word that continued to come into his mind this night. That was the one thing that he needed most of all, right now.

***

The boat was bouncing horribly. Jean Philippe leaned over the side and for the sixth time vomited. Abdul had braced Jacob in the long high-speed craft. Jacob was totally miserable, feeling as if he was being kicked in the ribs by a mule every minute or so. The night was clear so the smugglers had to travel at breakneck speed to get across the thirty miles that separated Turkey from Greece. They made this journey four times a week bringing in loads of cigarettes without tax stamps, liquor, and the occasional high priced passenger who just didn't seem to have the proper documents to gain entry into some countries. These men used the high-speed boats known in the trade as 'cigar boats'. These boats could travel over sixty miles an hour on rough seas and seventy-five on smooth water. It was not smooth tonight. A five-foot chop was running and these men were pushing their three-engine crafts for all they were worth. Gray water was flying back into the cockpit and everyone was wet.

The smuggler's boat ran with no lights and the hulls were painted a flat black. They had high-speed silencers on all engines that quieted them by half. But this was a journey that Abdul would never want to do again.

Hamill was piloting this boat. His friend, Gassort had taken the other boat down the coast off the northern border to meet an Israeli gunboat on picket duty. Gassort knew exactly where it was because he had been making the run for three years without detection. He told them that he could have the rest of the Israeli team back home by morning. Gassort had been smuggling luxury items into Israel for a group of businessmen who did not want to pay the taxes on those things. Jacob sat there and just listened as they described outrunning the border guards and coastal patrols with impunity.

Hamill had chosen to make the run to Greece because he knew that run the best. He told them that he could outrun the Turks which patrolled the coast but it was the Greek Navy that worried him because they were getting more sophisticated in their approach to stopping drug smugglers. Lately, they had taken up the practice of firing their seventy-five millimeter deck gun at boats that did not heave-to when approached. Hamill told them that this month, two boats had been blown out of the water and everyone aboard killed. In addition, they had lost a lot of fine American cigarettes. He spat overboard as he spoke of it.

"What happened to the days when they would confiscate your boat, send you home with a huge fine and smoke your cigarettes. Those days are gone. Now they believe everyone that smuggles is carrying drugs." He spat again. "I curse the drug runners. They are the scum of the earth. My family has been smuggling for two hundred years and never have we touched that trash. The authorities know that, but still they lump us all together. What are things coming to?" He pushed the boat harder. Abdul stood beside him and looked into the darkness of the sea that was all around him.

"Can you see anything out here?"

"No, can you?"

"Then how do you know where you are going?" Abdul felt the pain in his stomach again as the boat slammed into the water.

Hamill pointed at the small screen on the dashboard of the boat. "G. P. S." He spelled it out slowly for the other man. "American satellite system. . . very accurate. It positions us less than a meter from where we want to be. The only thing I have to do is control the speed and make sure those pigs from the Greek Navy don't find us." He pushed the three red knobs on the dash farther forward and Abdul hung onto the sissy-bar that ran across the whole width of the dashboard.

Abdul worked back toward where Jean Philippe was sitting and holding his stomach.

Abdul got down and spoke close to his ear. "How are you doing?"

"I am going to confess to anything they want me to confess to, if they promise to get me off of this boat and shoot me." Abdul slapped him on the back.

"Glad to hear you're doing well." Abdul worked back up to the small cabin where Jacob was holding onto the rails and gritting his teeth.

"You okay?" Abdul sat down next to him while lighting a cigarette and then handed it to the older man.

"Thank you." Jacob shook his head. "If you wanted to kill me, you could have shot me back in Istanbul. There was no reason to beat me to death in this boat. I would have preferred that." He smiled.

"This wasn't my idea, but it is a pretty night out there."

"Did you ever hear the expression that 'payback is a bitch'?" He looked in the dim light of the cabin at Abdul.

"Yes I have."

"When this is done, you must come to Israel and I will show you how in my youth I use to drive tanks through the desert." The older man reached out and held onto Abdul's arm for additional support just as the boat hit the next wave extra hard.

"Boy, right now that seems like a fun idea." He patted the other man and went up on deck.

Abdul found the cabin to be too confining and his stomach was working overtime. He stood again next to Hamill who was reducing speed. They were entering a small bay that showed no lights at all around the perimeter. "Where are we?"

"Greece. The Home of the World and the Land of the Blind Poet Homer. He immortalized my people in his epic, *The Iliad*." Hamill looked pleased with himself.

"Your people lost in that book. The Greeks burned Troy and killed your people."

"Oh shit, that was a long time ago, anyway." Hamill picked up a lamp and flashed the light in two series of three blips. The signal was answered by another light fifty meters away. Abdul could not even tell what was there or what the light was coming from.

"Okay, you're home free." Hamill moved the boat closer and a black seaplane loomed out of the darkness. "Get your friends and have a good life."

Abdul shook Hamill's hand and said nothing. He helped Jacob through the door of the waiting seaplane. Jean Philippe made it on his own and then folded up in the corner on a pile of bags. Within moments they were airborne and traveling west. Abdul checked the dressing on Jacob's leg and found it had started to bleed again. He tightened the bandage and pulled some painkillers out of his pocket. At first Jacob refused them, but finally gave in and took two pills. In a matter of minutes he was in a deep sleep. Abdul sat in the darkened interior of the plane and wondered if all of this was nearly over. He rolled up on his side in a tight ball and started to cry.

***

Father Leno sat at the desk and read through the rest of the brief. He needed security people to guard the Archbishop and he needed security people to cover the conclave on Friday. He also needed docents tomorrow to guide the tourist around the Vatican. Father Leno looked at the agenda for the meeting on Friday and shuddered. On that day, there would be a lot of people in the Papal Offices that didn't like each other. Needing one more favor to be called in, Leno picked up the phone and stared at it. This was going to be the most difficult. He was now following an order from someone else, under the authority of the Pope. Father Leno knew that this could still go very wrong for that Old Man upstairs because there were a lot of people who would not be happy with the changes around here, especially some Cardinals who had lined their pockets with Giovanni's money and had enjoyed a life that few mortals ever come to know. He did not worry about those forces outside the church for they probably did not yet know anything about what had transpired in the last forty-eight hours. Presently there were enough problems to be handled inside the grounds of the Vatican that required his undivided attention. He dialed the number and listened for the answer. This call was harder to make than the one he had placed to his brother in Sicily.

The voice on the other end was abrupt and gruff. Leno spoke not in his normal Italian but in French. He explained what he needed and what he would pay. Then he mentioned one of the two names on his list, the name of Him who had directed him to make this call. Upon hearing that, the answer came back down the line.

"Oui."

"Good, what do you need?"

"Clear it with the government and have papers ready at the airport in the morning."

"It has been cleared with the government and papers will be there and so will I."

He hung up and sat back. Not in six centuries had anybody in the Vatican committed to the actions that he had just taken. He closed his eyes and prayed to be right.

CHAPTER TWENTY-SIX

"Cry havoc and let slip the dogs of war."
"Julius Caesar" - William Shakespeare

The Papal limo was waiting at Rome's International Airport when the plane landed. It rolled to the private terminal and four men went out to help the three get off the plane and into the waiting car. The limo drove slowly around the airfield as it was not yet time to return to the Vatican. Father Leno looked at the plane's three passengers and noted the injuries.

"It looks as though you could use some cleaning up and some medical attention." Leno felt bad for all of them. He could not imagine what they had gone through and did not want to try.

"You ought to see us on a bad day." Jean Philippe smiled at the older priest.

"I think that is an honor I can live without." Leno understood the dark humor but still had trouble with it.

"Suite yourself, but it beats a desk job." Jean Philippe was feeling much better now that he was back on earth.

"Is His Holiness alright and did you apprehend Archbishop Giovanni?" It was the first time that Abdul spoke.

"His Holiness is concerned as we all are, but he is doing well. Thank you for asking. Archbishop Giovanni is being detained right now under the protection of the Pope. This action, you can imagine has caused some problems in the College of Cardinals, but I have him secreted away to where no one can get to him without my approval."

Leno allowed himself a small smile of personal triumph, more for the fact that he had put Giovanni's young sprat of an assistant in the worse place in the whole facility and left the two meanest men he had ever met to guard over him.

The limo drove down the tarmac toward the commercial freight area of the airport. The car stopped at the edge of one of the buildings. Leno looked outside at the building.

"I am going to leave you here. The other Fathers will assist you when you get back to the Vatican. Special rooms have been prepared for you in the area of the Papal Apartment. A doctor is standing by to tend to each of you, especially you, Mr. Isaac. But I have something else to do and I am needed there." He started to get out and then turned to remark. "As Chief of the Vatican Security I must ask each of you if you are still armed?"

Abdul expected Leno would want their guns. Nobody would get into the Papal Apartment area armed. He knew that.

"Yes. . . We all still have our guns." Abdul started to reach in the small of his back for his automatic.

"Good. Have a nice morning." With that he was out the door and into the building.

"Good?" Jean Philippe looked at the other two men.

"You know, I never knew how strange you people really are." Jacob put his pistol back into his pocket.

"Neither did I Jacob." Abdul crossed his arms and felt the large car accelerate down the ramp.

***

The tall officer was dressed in khakis and talking to two other men. He stood in front of a contingent of hard young men dressed in the battle tan of the French Foreign Legion's 2nd Para regiment. Father Leno walked up to him and extended his hand. The man in uniform saluted the priest and then reached out to shake hands. With the greetings exchanged the introductions were now complete. Then Leno met with the man's subordinates. Leno pulled out the orders he had worked on all night and passed them around so everyone could see what they were expected to do. He explained that it was a twenty-five minute ride from the airport to the Vatican and when they got there he wanted everyone in position as indicated; within minutes.

This action needed to be fast, before the members of the church community knew what was happening and before tourists got there for the day.

The two Italian government officials looked on and understood that these men where just passing through Rome under Papal orders. By the treaty of 1456, Italy could not stop the coming or going of anyone to the Vatican. It was clear the current government did not like it, but they also did not want to cause an international incident in the streets of Rome. One official explained that from the time they left the airport until they reached the Vatican, they could not stop. The only exceptions were at street corners with stop signs or lights, and they had to stop for all expectant mothers crossing the streets at intersections or not. With this the men in uniform laughed. Suddenly the tall man barked an order and the men grabbed their gear and loaded into the four trucks provided by the Italian army.

"This is to be quiet, Colonel." Leno looked at the man.

"Oui. Father it will be."

The trucks moved out with a jeep in front. The Colonel and his driver sat in front with Father Leno seated in the back with his robes blowing around him. An invading army had arrived. *'Invited'* in under a defacto arrangement with the Vicar of Rome, the Pope of the Catholic Church, who was now to be protected by the men of the 2nd Para, French Foreign Legion from Corsica. These armed men were trained in the ways of war and they came to the center of peace to make sure that *peace* would remain.

CHAPTER TWENTY-SEVEN

"I seem to be a verb."
Buckminister Fuller

Abdul walked into the well-appointed apartment that had been provided for him in the Vatican.

It had two large rooms, one for sleeping and the other an improvised office with a large desk, a chair, and three stacks of papers and documents that he had been working on before leaving on his latest adventure. These were the papers he had to finalize before Friday, which was tomorrow and then present them to the Conclave. He knew them by heart because they represented eighteen months of painstaking research. Abdul's documents and papers described a long and bloody history of subversion and greed, as well as power and destruction. He knew that everything hung on his presentation and that the actions this Pope had taken were unparalleled in the recent history of the church. If the College of Cardinals found that the Pope had overstepped his boundaries by these actions, they could call for council to bring him down and replace him. It had not been done in hundreds of years, but the Canon Law existed and if used, could shake the very foundations of the Church of Rome. If he did not convincingly present all the facts in the manner needed to persuade the Conclave to agree with this Pope, some of these men would go to any extreme to have Giovanni reinstated and move to evict the man who presently sat on the Chair of St. Peter. Politics is as old as the church but this was about power, influence, and money. A bad combination when it comes to deciding who will sit in that Holy Chair down the hall.

Abdul started by refreshing his memory on the material to be presented. He knew that time was the element. The Pope could not hold Giovanni for too long without allowing him contact with the outside world once the facts had come to light as to how and where the money had been moved. Giovanni would go to any lengths to get it back. He was the caretaker of a vast fortune of ill-gotten gains and there were those involved who would reach across time and space to make someone pay for their losses.

Abdul had just finished reading the first stack of documents, the ones he called the histories when he heard voices in the hallway raised in anger. His mind started to race. He wondered if it had already started the internal storming of the Winter Palace by the Cardinals. He put his handgun in the small of his back, pulled his sweater over it and then went to open the door.

"They can not be here, this is the Vatican!" A fat Cardinal dressed in the royal robes of the church was standing at the Pope's door through which the young assistant was blocking passage. "I must see him and tell him that foreign soldiers are on our grounds and he must make them go away."

Abdul approached the two men. Both men turned to see a large man with a purple scar running down the side of his face and recent injuries that covered the other side come nearer.

"Who is this?" The Cardinal spoke to the assistant.

"I am Father Lindquist, Proconsul to the Pontiff of Rome and Senior Advisor for Temporal Matters of the Church." Abdul leaned against the doorframe.

"Well whoever you are, this has nothing to do with you. So be gone, go away!"

"It has everything to do with me. My brief is the protection of the Church in the world and the security of the person of the Pope. If you've got a problem, you come to me." Abdul smiled at the man.

"I have never heard of you. Father Leno is head of security and as far as I know, no one holds the title to Protector of Temporal Matters." He backed off some but still wanted entrance to the Office of the Holy See.

"Father Leno and everyone else on this floor works for me with the exception of His Holiness. Now if you do not want to be forcibly carted off this floor, I suggest you go back to your office and do something worthwhile. . . like pray for your sins." Abdul turned to the young Priest. "Go back inside and assure His Holiness that he will not be disturbed again."

With that the Pope's assistant stepped back through the door and locked it behind him. The Cardinal stood there glaring at Abdul. "I remember now. You are the one who the Archbishop said wanted to assassinate His Holiness."

"Not bloody likely, Father. Now get off this floor before I drag your fat ass off it, myself."

"You lay a hand on me. . ."

Abdul grabbed the Cardinal by the front of his robe and pulled him close enough to smell his after-shave. "You don't have the balls or guts to threaten someone like me, 'cause you couldn't carry it out."

"I am a man of peace." The Cardinal was visibly shaken by the quickness and strength of the other man.

"Sure you are, Father."

"Sir!" A voice rose from the ascending staircase. "Is there a problem here?"

Abdul turned to see Colonel Michael Dupres, the Legion Commander walking towards them. When Abdul turned Dupres recognized him. "Father Lindquist, may I assist you?"

"Colonel, I want two of your best men stationed at the foot of this staircase. Nobody is to come up here without my explicit authorization. And would you be so kind as to take the Cardinal here. . . " Abdul brushed off the front of the Cardinal where he had grabbed him, "back down to his office and make sure he is comfortable."

"By all means. I will have my men here in two minutes. Anything else?" The Colonel was coldly eyeing the fat man in his scarlet robes.

"I need to speak with you later when you have a few moments, both you and Father Leno, if you please?"

"It would be an honor." He turned to the Cardinal and in excellent Italian asked him politely to leave the area which the other man did with haste. The Colonel leaned over and said to Abdul quietly, "I don't think actions like that will help your cause, chum."

Abdul smiled and pointed his chin at the retiring Cardinal hurrying down the staircase. "That one is already bought and paid for. He would not defend the Pope or hold to his vows of loyalty. . ." Abdul jerked his thumb toward the Pope's door, ". . . if the Virgin Mother, Herself was standing next to the Pope."

"I never knew that it was this bad in this place?" Dupres was looking up at the ornate ceiling and gilded walls.

"It is a jungle, Michael, draped with gold and purple maybe, but don't kid yourself. It is just as deadly here as what we saw years ago in Africa." Abdul put one large hand on the man's arm. "But then you were a shave-tail Lieutenant still wet behind the ears and just out of Military School."

"Yeah, that may be true, but your hair was black, not speckled with salt and pepper and you were much more handsome." Both men laughed.

Abdul's eyes grew serious as he looked at the other man with concern. "This is not over yet and it may get ugly. Leno did not want to call you because this will cause all kinds of hell in the press. So I hope you and your men understand that you are not window dressing."

"I figured that out just after Father Leno called and told me that the Holy Father and you personally had requested us. I brought my '*best boys*' that's all I can do. We are here to do what we do best, you know that, but I don't have any idea what we are up against?"

"None of us do yet, but the people that control Giovanni will not take this lying down. I am truly concerned for him." He pointed again at the Pope's door. "This takes more courage than I have. He is going up against a bunch of jackals, such as the one who was just here. Those I think he can handle, but it is the unknown. . . what Giovanni's people might try. If they can get to the Pope before the conclusion of the Conclave, this is a dead issue and so is everyone involved in it. The biggest problem we have is to keep the press out of it." He rubbed his face and pointed at the open door down the hallway. "That's my room. Come up when you get a chance and I will tell you everything I know."

"Sir." The Colonel stepped back and saluted the other man. He turned and walked down the staircase barking orders to the four men who had shown up at the bottom.

***

Jacob was in a conservative new suit provided by the Vatican's tailors. His wound had received medical care and he was walking with a fine ebony cane. He was looking at the paintings in the small side chapel off the main room of St. Peters. Walking next to Jacob was Jean Philippe dressed in his Roman blacks with a missionary collar. It is the uniform of a Brother of the Order, Society of Jesus, the Jesuits. He was shaven and his hair well trimmed. Jacob had noticed that it seemed as if the man had made a complete physical transformation from the hard, rough man he had watched fight twenty four hours previously.

"You know most of these paintings were stolen from countries all over Europe?" Jacob pointed with his cane to a beautiful example of late Flemish art on the wall.

"Rubbish." Jean Philippe was carrying a small black prayer book in his hand. He spoke in the lowest of tones out of respect for their location.

"You guys claim that everything was stolen, probably from your family when they were driven out of east rusty nut somewhere."

"Ours is a history of evictions." Jacob continued to walk and sneered at some of the more gross religious works on the wall.

"All you had to do was embrace the 'true' faith and you could have stayed and continued to charge the Lords and Nobles of their countries interest in huge percentages." Jean Philippe was enjoying this game of who could get the better of each other.

"Embrace the 'true' faith. Bah!" He pointed toward the chairs that had been set aside for those who wished to sit and meditate in the small room. "We have been practicing our faith for five thousand years success-fully. Look at this. . ." He pointed to a gold candle-stand sitting on the side of the altar, "probably stolen by the Crusader Knights from Solomon's temple."

"No. I think that one was stolen from the Sultan of Cairo. He had better gold." Jean Philippe looked around the empty room and then sat down.

"The Egyptians stole it from us in the third century. I know about these things." Jacob smiled as he looked up at the paintings and the wood-work on the walls. "I never thought I would be sitting here and seeing all of this. I have never considered coming to Rome to look around. . . it was not something that I would normally have done."

"Too busy being a spy?" Jean Philippe closed his eyes for a moment.

"A patriot!"

"That too." Jean Philippe noticed that the man never sat still. He was constantly moving and watching.

"What are we doing here?" He looked at Jean Philippe.

"Are we just looking at old, bad, stolen pictures of religious scenes which mean nothing to the world today."

"You know what I mean. . . I am ordered here by my boss and I am be-ing babysat by a walking contradiction." He turned to Jean Philippe fully. "Do you have any idea what this is about?"

"Yes I do."

"Can you tell me something, so I won't go just stark raving mad?" The frustration had built up again in Jacob.

"Abdul must present the case for the Pope tomorrow. Oh, there will be others to assist him, learned doctors of the church and theologians, scholars, historians, but all of that is window dressing. The Pope has a plan to change some things in the church and somehow you are part of that. The second issue is. . . that all of us know that at any time, something can go terribly wrong. That is why these fine young men from Corsica are here. No one could have got to them yet.

"But mostly, I think before this conclave is over, Abdul believes someone will try and kill His Holiness. So if that is the case, Abdul wants us and the legionnaires to be close at hand. We are the only ones that he trusts."

"That is all well and good, but I don't know you people." Jacob rubbed his leg. "I was thrown into this. I do not understand any of this and yet I am in the middle of it all. It does not make sense to me, and no one is returning my calls from Israel." He put his hands up in supplication to a higher power.

"Jacob, you represent the outside world. You are not Catholic and not one of us, but you can bear witness to the events and facts that are going to be given here tomorrow. If you know them, then it is presumed that your country will know. And no one is going to be able to disavow Israel standing up and talking about all of this. We may be strangers, but I know that we are connected in this, otherwise Abdul would not have you here." Jean Philippe realized that he sounded more like a priest than he cared too. "I have told you all that I know. Anything else would be speculation or just a lie. I am good at those." Jean Philippe smiled.

"And I thought the backstreets of Beirut were bad? Come on. . . Show me some more of the stolen artifacts that belonged to my family." Jacob got up and started to walk into the main area of the Church of St. Peter's.

***

The man sat at the desk and read the letter for the third time. He understood its contents but he was having a hard time understanding the reasoning behind it. He was not allergic to the idea of killing. In fact it was his trade. His had been a lifetime in the business of ending human life and he had enjoyed the rewards of this existence. A beautiful home on the coast overlooking a magnificent bay with fine wine, beautiful women and fast cars, all of which had been paid for by those who wanted someone else gone. He read the bottom of the letter again. "You will probably be arrested and charged with the crime, but we have made arrangements to get you out of the jail and safely out of the country. No one will know who you are. This will require up-close and in-tight work. There can be no chance of escape. So don't even try. Surrender to the authorities at once on the completion of the task." The assassin had never seen such a stipulation. But then again he had never seen such an offered payment. He looked at the documents and identifications that had been provided to him. They would get him in anywhere. But this was not the type of job he wanted to do, for just anyone. The rest of the letter provided him with no other options. "If you choose not to do this for us, consider our arrangement at an end."

That was as good as telling him that if he didn't do this, he too was a dead man. The killer looked at the woman swimming in the pool on his terrace. Her nude body moved through the water effortlessly. He watched her long hair flow behind her as she did laps. He closed the letter and picked up the phone.

"Yes, hello. Please book me a flight this afternoon." He listened to the other end.

"Rome." He sat for a moment and thought about all of this.

"No, just for one. Returning? Let's leave it an open ticket for now."

CHAPTER TWENTY-EIGHT

*"Fridays are feared by many people, especially when the Friday is the 13*th *day of the month, for it was on this day that Phillip the Fair, King of France, destroyed the power and the wealth of the Knights Templars."*
History of Superstitions

The Conclave had been assembled in the Papal Office on the morning of Friday, the thirteenth day of the month in July. With all the pomp of a coronation they had come, the six members of the Holy College of Cardinals in their robes, white gloves, and rings of station. The Pope sat in his whites in the large chair on the dais at the head of the room. Two large dark wooden tables had been prepared for the two opposing groups who would present all the facts. In the back of the room were four professors from the Vatican University. Their task was to translate between French, Italian and for one special guest, Hebrew. Twenty-five members of major departments were allowed to enter the chamber to observe. Along with sixteen other members of the church who had been brought from various parts of Europe to be available if their skill or knowledge were needed. The only unusual attendees in the room were the eight Paratroopers from the French Foreign Legion that stood at attention in assigned locations.

Jacob and Jean Philippe sat at a side table flanked by two scribes who were to take notes and be their assistants. A Vatican transcription expert sat near the front of the room, much like a court recorder. The outside hallway had been closed and in fact the entire central administrative complex of the Vatican had been shutdown. The Paratroopers were polite but firm with all those seeking access to the Conclave. Without the proper credentials, no one was going to get into the building. It was silent in the hallways and only whispered conversation was used in the offices that were occupied. All civilian personnel had been given an extra day off for the weekend, so only the clergy were working. Everyone wanted to know what was going on. What the results of this meeting would be and how it would affect the operations of the Vatican.

At 9:00 A. M. Archbishop Giovanni and his two assistants were ush-ered into the room by Father Leno and two very hard-looking young Para-troopers. They were directed to sit at a table on the right facing the Pope. All of them appeared in simple cassocks with no adornments of church rank or position.

Before Giovanni sat, he surveyed the table across from him where Abdul sat with three other priests.

"I shall not sit here with this murderer. I will not be judged by this tribunal nor will I accept any sentence passed by it."

The Pope sat and listened carefully. Then he motioned for Giovanni to sit; which he would not.

"Father Giovanni. . . this is not a trial of secular law. We are not judging your innocence or guilt for any action that you have taken. I have convened this Conclave for the express purpose of allowing a select num-ber of the College of Cardinals to hear the evidence put forth regarding actions that affect the operations of this City-State and this Church. My decision has already been made and those facts offered to the members of this panel. They wish to hear only the precipitating facts or events that led to this determination on my part. If you do not care to participate in this Conclave, you do not have to. However, if you chose not to. . . you are in direct conflict with this Pope. I will have no other choice but to defrock you, here and now, and have you escorted from the grounds of this Holy Place. You will leave here a common citizen of Italy with all the rights and privileges of that status. But know if you stay, you have sworn an oath of loyalty and service to this Church and to me as Head of this Church." Before the Holy Father could continue, Giovanni interrupted.

"That is exactly what I wish, as do my assistants." He turned to see all of them nod in agreement with him. "We wish to be released at once."

"I would however, like to finish with my opening statement, which may offer to you a little more insight before you make such a choice."

"I don't think you can say a thing that would make me feel any dif-ferent after the indignities that I have had to suffer."

"I think I might have one or two things that will affect your decision." The Pope closed his hands on his lap to make himself more comfortable in the chair and sat in silence. A mummer ran through the collected group of Cardinals. One of whom was a member of the inner ring of Giovanni's influence, as both the Pope and Giovanni knew. The Cardinal stood and spoke quietly. "Father Giovanni, it would be prudent for you to hear all that His Holiness has to say before you commit yourself and others to action that could be seen as placing your person and soul in great jeopardy." The Cardinal returned to his seat. Giovanni looked carefully at the man and tried to estimate what he had meant. Giovanni had long given up on his soul, but the reference to his person caught him off-guard. He decided to sit and waved for them to continue on.

The Pope continued. "We have asked Father Lindquist, who is our Proconsul to prepare documents that have brought together the information leading us to our actions. I have requested that copies of all the information be made available during his discourse so that each of the Cardinals and specific others in this room can follow the references that he makes. Again, I must state that this is not a Court of Civil Law, but rather one of Canon Law. Some of the information for the sake of clarification is historical in nature and must be offered here without comment.

"If you and your assistants wish to participate in this session, you are required by Decorum and Rules of the Conclaves to listen without interruption. Do you all so acknowledge?" The Pope repositioned himself in his chair to get comfortable again.

Giovanni turned to his fellow priests and conferred quietly. They all nodded in agreement. Giovanni started to think that maybe they did not have much evidence to present and this was an effort by the Pope to regain some of the power he had lost to the Office of Special Congregations. If so and if the evidence was inconclusive or faulty, this would only strengthen Giovanni's push to replace this *Old Has-Been*. If at the end of this Conclave they had nothing and what was there could be refuted, it would look very bad for the Pope. The only thing that Giovanni believed they could produce as evidence was the package that he had bought from Abdul and the implications could be redirected to suggest he had acted to protect others by securing the package's contents from being used to perhaps kill people. It would also be the basis of impeaching Abdul as a fine upstanding member of the church community. Giovanni quickly weighed the possibilities for winning against losing and thought his chances were very good.

"I only ask at the end of the presentation that I am allowed to offer some form of defense for any actions that I have taken." Giovanni had risen from his chair and addressed the Cardinals and then the Pope.

"You will be permitted to add anything that you would like to at the end of Father Lindquist's presentation." The Pope was careful not to use the words defense or evidence.

As Giovanni sat back down, no one noticed the middle-aged man with graying hair enter the back of the room. He had presented his documents to the Paratrooper at the door, who inspected them and then pointed to an open chair. The man sat and looked at the two priests to his right and nodded.

He made the sign of the cross and bent his head in silent prayer.

***

Abdul Hassan, Abdul the Bandit, or in his present presentation, Father Raoul Dominic Lindquist, Ph.D., S. J., stood and addressed the Pope and the collection of Cardinals. The rules of decorum within the church were old and the traditions around them dated from the Middle Ages. Abdul knew them as well as he did Canon Law. He wanted to present the information in a concise and unbroken line from beginning to end with conclusions and actions implemented at the very end. He stood there for a moment, bowed his head and then started:

"In the autumn of 1934 the Office of Special Congregations (OSC) was formed. It came into existence due to pressures in the world. Europe was undergoing vast changes and the spread of fascism was remapping the face of Europe. Italy had been under the reins of a dictator for almost twelve years and this period also saw the rise of Adolf Hitler in Germany. For the Church to survive it needed some way of dealing with these temporal situations without having it affect the body of the Church. . ."

"Excuse me. . ." all eyes turned to the Cardinal who supported Giovanni. Rules of protocol allowed any of the Cardinals to interrupt and ask questions at any point. Abdul gestured to the Cardinal to have his say. Knowing he could be disrupted at each phase of the presentation suggested that it was going to be a long day.

"What does this have to do with the Archbishop? He was not yet born."

"This is background, Your Eminence, it is necessary to know about these facts to see how they effect current actions." Abdul knew this kind of tactic would be employed, but he had not imagined that it would start this early.

"Yes, yes, but we are all very aware of the *what happened during the forties.* Can we not shorten this by discussing relevant facts about today?" The high nasal voice of the Cardinal was showing his condescension and his impatience with all of this, a reaction that Abdul had prepared for.

"Your Eminence, can you tell me about the Odessa, or the Rat Line, or say who Skorzeny was?"

Abdul waited and looked at the man.

"No, should I know about these things? They are not of this Church."

"But they are and if you will indulge me a little, I will explain what they are and how they have greatly affected this Church then, and now.

Jacob's ears had perked up. He looked at Abdul and wondered what any of this had to do with the Conclave. The Odessa, the Rat Line and Skorzeny were issues he knew about and wanted to know more. He turned and looked at Jean Philippe. Jean Philippe kept his blank stare fixed on the Cardinal.

"Please proceed, but I must ask that you keep this relevant to the present. If you must cite history please do so quickly."

The Cardinal sat down and Giovanni smiled slightly. He knew that the Cardinal would make it difficult for the presentation to include anything but relevant issues.

"Thank you for your counsel." Abdul said flatly and picked up his brief again. "During the Second World War, the Office of Special Congregations had its agents working at the highest levels in both Germany and Italy. On the surface they were operating to maintain freedom of practice for Catholics living in those two countries and in the occupied regions of Europe.

But the records shows," he pointed to one of the assistants to hand out the first set of prepared documents, "that they were in fact, aiding the Reich in its plan for future conquest. These papers have been removed from the Archive of the Office of Special Congregations and show dates, times, meetings and the agendas of those meetings. For interceding with certain Swiss banking organizations, the Church helped provide the Germans and the Italians with a place to move money and buy items they could not get from anybody else in the world. This continued throughout the war years.

In this second set. . . you will notice," Abdul again pointed to the assistant to hand them out, "that there are documents which notified the Church through the Office of Special Congregations of what was happening to the Jews in Germany, as well as the Gypsies, Slavs, Poles, and any who disagreed with the Reich. By 1942 we knew that people were being killed by the thousands in death camps. This information was concealed inside the Office of Special Congregations and never given to the Church authorities."

Jacob pulled out his notebook and started to make notes. He looked at the documents handed to him and thanked the young priest. Then he opened them and looked at the many records of correspondence between the top men in Germany and the members of the Office. He could not believe that these papers even existed. He rubbed his face. This is not what he had expected today to hear in this room.

"Father Lindquist . . . I understand the importance of this to history, but. . ."

"Enough, Cardinal!" The Pope raised a hand. "It will not work. There will be no more delays in this presentation. Sit down now, listen and learn." The rebuke from the Pope was enough to silence the man. He returned to his seat.

Without hesitation, Abdul continued. "When the war was finally winding down and they knew that they had lost, the Nazis came back to their old friends in the OSC and asked for further assistance. The OSC provided more than ten thousand false documents, travel papers and diplomatic visas for war criminals to the top Nazis' and civilians who would have otherwise been caught up in the dragnet after the war. They got out of Germany and spread throughout the world. Throughout Germany and its occupied regions, they had collected stolen loot from the death camps, banks and repositories. This amounted to hundreds of millions of dollars. Much of it was sent through the Church's accounts to be held in trust for the people like the Perons' of Argentina fame. This *underground railroad* which aided in the escape of those men and their stolen money was known as the Rat Line. Document batch three shows names, dates, amounts paid to the OSC for services and where those people went." The next portfolio was presented to the nods of the Cardinals and others in the room. Giovanni was looking down at the floor. He knew all of this but he could not understand how they were going to prove his involvement. Abdul continued, "Otto Skorzeny, an SS Colonel, was responsible for setting up the money route. He was head of a group called the Odessa which was an enterprise established to protect former SS officers after the war. Neither Skorzeny nor the rest of those men could get the banking done anyplace where the allies had influence. So he went back to his friends at the OSC and had them become the bankers/brokers for the SS and Odessa. From 1945 to 1952, approximately four hundred million U. S. dollars were pumped through the Office into Swiss bank accounts to be held for and used by the Odessa or any group who came after. Its principal use was to protect former SS men in hiding. However as time went by, it started to be used to set up businesses and other enterprises that were, shall we say, not completely honorable. Genetic research firms were formed, chemical and biological laboratories established, all with the same underlining goal, the genocide of the Jewish people. Monies poured into Arab countries to help splinter groups and overthrow moderate leaders, so that more radical anti-Semitic powerbrokers could continue the work started in the forties by the Nazis.

By the late sixties the OSC had become a vast network of secret organizations, all funded by stolen gold. By this time most of the old SS men were gone, they had died, given up, moved away, changed names, whatever, but a subtle new force was emerging from the new lands and wealth of the Middle East, people that shared the goal of Jewish elimination, but for different reasons. The OSC fostered those relationships and its coffers grew. Promoting itself as a center of commerce for anyone that had a special need, it is estimated that thirty-five different rightwing, anti-Semitic and Radical organization's monies found a safe home with the banker of the Special Office. . . and always for a price, a small percentage of the monies being moved."

Abdul paused and took up the next file. He opened it and motioned to the younger priest to hand out the next group of documents. "In 1975, His Eminence the Archbishop Giovanni took over the Office. This was after ten years of working in the shadow of the previous Archbishop, much as his present assistants work for him. He started at the edge and worked into the position of Head of the Office. He moved the business enterprise into high gear. He collected monies, moved them, increased the percentage taken and all the time put money back into other pockets that would aid him in his dealings. This next set of documents shows the groups that have deposited the monies with him and in the same portfolio you will find a list of payments made to Officials in government, politics and in this very facility. All of the names have been double checked for accuracy and the pathway used to pay them has been traced."

"Where in the hell did you get these?!" Giovanni was holding the documents in his trembling hands and shouting. "These are my private files!"

"Priests do not have private files here in the Vatican." The Pope spoke in his normal quiet tone.

"But these are not concerning the Church, these are my own. . ."

"These records were found on your computer. . . which is owned by the Church and in your office which the Church lets you use." Abdul never looked over at the Archbishop but continued.

"Two years ago, some disturbing information came forward as a result of a fine Jewish scholar's work, Professor Moshe Bergman. Through the efforts of his government and with help from the governments of America, France and England, he had researched and found where hundreds of millions of stolen dollars had been lodged in Swiss accounts. The Swiss finally gave up the money to be returned to survivors of the holocaust. Some 25,000 to 113,000 people fit into this group of remaining survivors. But Bergman had gone further. He had traced four hundred million dollars of Reich funds that had disappeared. Not surprisingly, you may notice in document number one, that this is exactly the amount that the Office of Special Congregation's bank account starts with. So in conclusion to this part of the presentation, I believe that we have shown that from the beginning of the Office until now, the directors have mismanaged, used and abused power to build a financial empire not for the Church, but for themselves." Abdul sat down and rested for a few moments.

The one Cardinal who had been so insistent on defending the Archbishop was stuck on one page; the one that listed those inside the Vatican that had taken money. His name headed the list. They had the amounts, his bank account numbers, and how much he had used. The Cardinal closed his eyes and thought that maybe, just maybe, he could get through this if he distanced himself from the Archbishop and personally pleaded ignorance to the Holy Father.

The Pope declared a recess in the proceedings for half an hour. Two Legionnaires escorted the Archbishop and his group out into a small room off the hallway that had been set aside just for them.

Jacob walked up to Abdul and held up the documents. "May I have these?"

"Of course. That is why I wanted you here to see this and to be given those."

"That is the only reason?" Jacob looked puzzled.

"No, there is something else, but that is for His Holiness to speak about, not me."

Jacob grasped the man's arm and looked long and hard into his eyes. "I would not have believed that you are such a good man."

"I'm not." He smiled. "It's just an act."

"Damn good one, then." Jacob returned to his seat.

"See, the whole place does belong to my family." Jacob was speaking out of the corner of his mouth to Jean Philippe who was still goading him.

"Not yet. You may own the lower level of the men's room on the first floor, but not the Museum and that is where all the really good stuff is." Jean Philippe rubbed his hands as he watched the collection of men who were discussing the documents and the paperwork among themselves. He noticed that Giovanni's defending Cardinal had left the room by the side door and was nowhere to be seen.

Abdul walked over to their table and leaned down to look at Jean Philippe. "You ready?"

"No. But I will give it my best effort." He got up and walked to the Proconsul's table and looked through the notes. He discussed two issues with the theologians and historian who were all shaking their heads in agreement. The Pope returned from his apartment and asked everyone to be seated and then asked that the other men be returned. Giovanni was not walking as proudly as before. He could not believe that they had penetrated his world to such a depth. He was at the moment considering options. He could leave the Church and continue to function as a middle-man for some of the groups because he had developed enough banking relationships over a quarter of a century to allow this. He thought at this point that his chances for the Chair of St. Peter were getting slimmer by the moment. He noted that the only Cardinal that had supported him was gone and it did not look like he was coming back. Well, Giovanni thought, we will deal with him later.

When everything had quieted down and everyone was in his place, the Pope started the second session. "Brothers, now I must ask Brother Baptiste to explain what actions have been taken under '*my*' direct order?" He gestured toward Jean Philippe, who rose.

"We needed proof that Canon Law has been violated and that the person of His Holiness was in danger. A year ago a plan was developed to offer to the OSC a way that they could deal with the outcry of the State of Israel and Jews from around the world who also wanted to know what complicity the Church had played in the Nazis' escape schemes and the actions that came after. Audits had been ordered of known Vatican bank accounts and the Council of World Jewry was presented with the information. It did not please them. The old story of a cover up surfaced again. The pressure was mounting for the last twenty-two months for a more thorough investigation of monies controlled by the Church. When the OSC came back to His Holiness and told Him that there was nothing in any accounts that had come via the Nazis, the Holy See decided to go a different route.

This is when Father Lindquist and I were brought in. Our efforts showed a direct line to the Office and that it controlled vast wealth which was unreported to the Vatican's Minister of Finance. It was determined that the only way we could discover the truth was by placing someone inside the Office of the Special Congregation to obtain facts and figures. And in an effort to protect him, we asked the Vatican's Head of Security, Father Leno, to electronically penetrate the office. This he did, but all the information that Father Leno provided we had already because Father Marcus was working with us. He provided us with files, computer print-outs and all the needed information as well as being our intermediary to the Holy Office while we were working in the field."

Father Marcus got up and walked to one side of the room and sat back down next to Jacob. Giovanni glared at the man. Leno looked shocked and bewildered. He had thought this man a weakling and suddenly he is center stage in this performance.

Jean Philippe continued, "Without him, the three of us," he pointed to Abdul, himself and Jacob, "would be dead men, along with some other fine young Israelis. He gave us facts, information and even names of those assigned to hunt and kill us in the Swiss Guards.

Next, when we requested that, His Holiness had Father Leno move all monies out of the accounts controlled by the Office. We knew. . ."

"You moved the money? It was not yours to move!" Giovanni was standing and shouting at the top of his voice. "They will think I did it. Without that money I am a dead man and they won't stop."

"Archbishop. . . compose yourself." The Pope pointed at him.

"Compose myself! You have just placed me under a death sentence. . . you senile old bastard."

One of the Paratroopers started to move to restrain him when a movement in the back of the room caught Abdul's eye. One of the priests was standing and from under his robe he had pulled a pistol.

Abdul leaped to the front of the room and threw himself in front of the Pope. Jacob had pulled his weapon and was trying to get an angle for a shot. All of the other people in the room were standing and moving around which was blocking his path of sight.

The roar of the priest's gun exploded in the gold gilded room. Abdul reflexed as he believed he had been hit. Jean Philippe in one turning motion brought his gun up just as the priest dropped his weapon. Jean Philippe fired four times. All of the slugs hit the man in his chest, ripping out his back. The assassin priest was dead before he hit the ground. Jean Philippe turned and saw Abdul covering the Pope. He looked down next to him to see Archbishop Giovanni on the floor with a clean round hole in his forehead. The guards were ushering people out of the room. Jean Philippe knelt and touched the throat of the Archbishop. He turned and looked at Abdul and shook his head — the man was dead. Jacob walked to the center of the room and looked at the scene.

"Who the hell is that?" Jacob pointed at the dead priest.

"I don't know, but we need to check his papers and see if he worked for the Archbishop." Jean Philippe put his gun away. Jacob walked over and pulled out the man's document case and read them. "Says he is Proctor of Archives at St. Simon's."

"The Proctor of Archives is about a thousand years old and deaf as a wall." Abdul walked up and looked at the papers. "Nobody would know that. . . would they? Our boys outside would think that he had every right to be here and was on the list with ten or twelve other Elders in the Church who did show up."

The Pope walked over and bent down next to the Archbishop to give him *Last Rights*. Father Marcus did the same for the false priest. When finished the Pope got up and looked at the other man. "He would have killed me."

Simultaneously Abdul and Jean Philippe answered, "Yes!" "No!"

The Pope looked confused at their contradictory answers. Abdul was first to speak. "His shot was dead-on where he intended it. He was after the Archbishop."

"I don't think so. The Archbishop just got caught in the crossfire. Too many people moving. And in all the action, he turned and wham. . . he got popped. Just as well because it saves us a lot of work."

"We will never know." All of them turned to Jacob who had just spoke. "The truth died there on that floor. All of it." Jacob walked away and out of the room.

"What did he mean by that?" Jean Philippe followed the man with his eyes.

"Exactly what he said." Abdul helped the Pope back to his room. Father Leno who had been standing by the windows walked over to Jean Philippe and looked at him. Then he turned and walked away without saying a word.

CHAPTER TWENTY-NINE

"And when the prophecy of your first transgression came to be fulfilled,
We sent against you a formidable army which ravaged your land
and carried out the punishment you had been promised."
Holy Koran - Book of the Night Journey

Saturday morning had passed quickly. Reports had been written and actions explained. Abdul sat in his room and finally felt that all of this was over. He had a nagging sensation at the back of his mind, but he thought that it would resolve itself, or perhaps it may not. He pushed the thought away. He had bundled up all his papers and turned them over to the historian who had come by to get them earlier in the morning. He sat at his desk with a cup of coffee and finally decided he could enjoy a moment's peace. The door opened and the young priest assigned to him came in and stood waiting to be acknowledged.

"What may I do for you?" Abdul realized that he frequently forgot protocol. He needed to work on that. He told himself, and then smiled.

"His Holiness would like you to join him in his room." The young man was looking at the carpet.

"When?"

"As soon as possible." The young acolyte turned and left without further conversation.

"I once had a dog like that. I loved that dog." Abdul got up and put his coat on. He picked up his pistol and held it for a moment. After opening the desk drawer he placed the pistol inside and closed it. He had walked halfway across the room and then went back. He opened the desk drawer again and picked up the gun. There was no hesitation to him placing it in the small of his back.

"I liked that dog a lot. . ."

As Abdul entered the large white and gold trimmed room, he noticed Jacob and Jean Philippe sitting there in quiet conversation. In a fun sort of way, they were becoming masters at seeing who could get the better of the other.

"Have I missed the party?" Abdul walked over and sat down.

"It has not started. The guest of honor is not here yet." Jean Philippe motioned toward the doorway that led into the Pope's private rooms.

"Oh, so we are just hanging out and swapping war stories." He smiled again, something he had not done in a long time.

"Do you take anything serious?" Jacob looked at him with some disgust.

"Sure. When Agassi or Sampras is winning at the French Invitational, I get really serious. . ."

His conversation was interrupted by the Pope's entrance into the room. The Pope motioned for them to stay seated. An assistant moved another chair over to the area where the men where sitting. The Pope joined them.

"This has been a trying period, gentlemen." Each man nodded his agreement with the profound but simple words of the man.

"Now we have some final business to handle." He placed his glasses on his nose and opened his notebook.

"First, Jean Philippe Emanuel Baptiste, you have done services for this Old Man, who few could have done. However, your task is not finished." He looked over his glasses at Jean Philippe. "How long have you and I known each other?"

"Since I was a boy and you used to come and visit Papa. You were a Bishop then and in all those years we have somehow stayed in contact." Jean Philippe smiled.

"I remember his studio in Paris. The smell of varnish and lacquer was wonderful. Oh, the things he could do with old broken musical instruments! It was truly a miracle." The Pope was recollecting different times with pleasure. "We have one of the finest instrument collections in the world in our museum, none of which anyone has heard in three hundred years or so. I would like you to become the Curator of musical instruments in the museum and start to repair some of them. I want to hear the sounds of *Bach* or *Beethoven* on a woodwind that was built during one of those great composer's times. I want to enjoy the sounds from one of their written works of art."

"Oh, but I have my shop in Paris. I have customers and my Mama still loves it there. . ."

The Pope laid a hand on Jean Philippe's leg to silence him. "I am sorry to tell you this, but your shop in Paris is no longer. It was consumed in a fire three days ago. Tragic, but that is the way some things happen. However, you will like it here. We have a wonderful little house just off the grounds where you and your mother can live until both of you are in heaven. A small but reasonable salary will be paid to you and plus as a personal pleasure, I would appreciate your company once in a while."

Jean Philippe was still digesting the fact that his shop was gone. "If that is Your Holiness's wish, who am I to object?" He felt as though he was put under house arrest, but it seemed as though the chains were velvet lined.

"Good." He looked at his notes. "Oh, that Clifford safe you put so much stock in?"

"Yes?"

"It took about seven minutes to open. One of Father Leno's people from Sicily did it." The Pope smiled a sardonic smile.

"The truffles?" Jean Philippe looked at Abdul who was intently studying the pattern on the carpet.

"He did not give you truffles, Jean Philippe. It was the biological warfare agent, described. . ."

The Pope saw it coming and raised a hand to Jacob before he could speak.

Jacob turned to Abdul and started . . . "You lied to me. . ."

"You would have thought more about the vector than the mission." Abdul stated.

"Please, Mr. Isaac, don't concern yourself." Jacob started to speak only to be stopped by the Pope again with a raised hand. "Two hours after we retrieved them, they were on their way to a laboratory in Israel to be analyzed to determine how best to defend against such things in the future." The Pope looked at his notes. Jacob did not know if he should be mad or grateful.

"Does any one of you not lie?"

"No." The Pope looked at him seriously. "We have had to, for the sake of our Church and your people. I understand your concern, but we are trying to make everything right. You will see."

"My pardon." Jacob sat back and looked at Abdul and shook his head in disbelief.

"Now as for you, Mr. Isaac, I have something for you." The Pope handed him an envelope.

"No, I need nothing but to go home. Thank you but no, please."

"It is not from me; it is from your superior." He pushed the letter toward Jacob, who opened it and read it before starting to laugh. "I have been fired. . . Forced into retirement because I helped you two in Turkey. Can you believe that?"

"Yes." It was the Pope that spoke. He held up another document. It carried with it the *Seal of the Holy Catholic Church* next to what looked to Jacob as the *Seal of the State of Israel.* "You were fired so that you can take up your new position. Here, read this." The Pope handed him the document. Jacob was smiling when he started to read it and then slowly his face started to turn into a frown. Then he started to cry. "I do not deserve this. I am not the one."

"Yes you are. It has been proven a hundred times over." The Pope looked at the other two men and touched Jacob's knee. "Mr. Isaac has been appointed Head of the Joint Catholic-Jewish Foundation, set up exclusively to use monies from a special account for only three things — educational programs, health programs and the arts. Even though it is a joint foundation, Mr. Isaac has total control. No one, not even myself nor anyone in Israel can override his decisions."

Jean Philippe grinned like a child. "That is wonderful, Jacob. Congratulations!"

Jacob tried to speak but his words failed him. He pointed to the heading on the page. Jean Philippe immediately understood his reaction. The new foundation was to be known as the *Ann Isaac Foundation.* Jacob kissed the Pope's hand and the Pontiff in turn embraced him.

"Old men do not need to retire, they just need to help the younger members of society learn from our mistakes." The Pope was looking at the man with a glow of joy.

"This is the money from the Jews that died in Germany?" Jean Philippe asked.

"Not quite." The Pope looked at his notes. "There was about 400 million in 1945 dollars. The accounts have grown some, since then."

"How much does my best friend in the world control?" Jean Philippe nudged Jacob who caught the reference.

"Approximately 17 billion dollars."

"Did I ever tell you that I have a lot of Jewish blood in me? I think we must also be first cousins also." Jean Philippe was hugging a beaming Jacob.

"Not a dime to him. That is the only rule which I will hope to impose on you, Mr. Isaac." They all laughed.

"Now if you two will excuse me, I need just a few moments alone with Father Lindquist." Both men got up, shook the Pope's hand and walked toward the door. As a final note the Pope turned and said. "Please just wait outside. Father Lindquist will be with you shortly." They nodded.

When the room was empty he closed his notebook and looked at Abdul. "Have you made peace with all of this and what you have had to do?"

"As best I can." He sat there leaning forward looking at the floor.

"You have certain Acts of Contrition that you must perform if you wish to remove all the sins that you have accumulated in the last few months." The Pope looked deeply into the man's eyes.

"Don't we all, Your Holiness?" Abdul sat back and met the man's gaze equally.

"Of course, but let us first start with the servant and not the master." Sternness clipped the Pope's words.

"Yes, Your Holiness."

"I first must ask you. . . do you still believe in all of this?" He gesture took in the room and more, indicating the Vatican and thus the Church.

"If I had not, would I have done any of this?"

"All right, then you also believe in our systems and its rules?"

"Of course."

"Then you will accept my rule here on earth as final?"

"Of course."

"Good. I have three penances for you to do. Will you accept them without question?"

"Yes, Your Holiness."

"First!" The Pope turned and called to his assistant who entered from another room with a box. The Pope opened it and indicated for Abdul to stand. He wrapped a Bishop's red sash around Abdul's waist and then placed a Bishop's signet ring on his finger. Abdul looked bewildered.

The Pope thanked his assistant and asked him to leave.

"Second! Within three months I want you to become the Rector of the Ecole of St. Martin's in Paris. I want you to build an excellent school out of it again. One the Church can be proud of once more." Abdul nodded again, without words.

"And finally! I want you to find it in your heart to forgive yourself. I have given you absolution from the Church for all deeds, but that to you is meaningless unless you forgive yourself."

"That is harder than you think."

"You accepted my rule over you, did you not?"

"Yes."

"Then I wish you to do this for me. For us all." Abdul hung his head and when he raised it again the Pope thought he detected a hint of a tear in the other man's eye.

Abdul softly replied, "I need you to do something for me, also. I think it may help in my returning to the human race." Abdul took a photograph out of his pocket. "When you celebrate *High Mass* tomorrow and announce the founding of the relationship between the Church and Israel, could you say a special blessing for her?" Abdul handed the Pope the picture he had taken from the effects of the dead girl in Paris. It seemed like three lifetimes and a million years ago.

"Did you know her well?" The Pope took the photo and looked at it.

"No, but she reminded me of someone long ago and there was no one to say mass for her in Paris, when she died."

"What was her name, Father?"

"Nicole. . . That is all I know. She was an art student that got into trouble and had a bad ending."

The Pope turned and pushed his button for one of the assistants to come. He handed him the photograph and said, "I would like that photo enlarged. It should be placed on the side altar at this Sunday's mass and I want a ribbon across it that reads 'Our Beloved Nicole'." He turned back to Abdul who stood up and they embraced one another.

Without another word both men walked back to their worlds.

***

When Abdul walked into the corridor both other men looked in amazement. Jacob was the first to speak, "They made you a Cardinal?"

"A Bishop. . . it is a little lower on the feeding order."

"You would think he would make me one also since he is my second cousin." Jean Philippe was holding the end of the Red sash and looking at the ring.

"You're not even ordained?"

"Yes, but I am related and you're a gunman for hire. Everyone knows that. . . don't they?" He looked to Jacob for confirmation. Jacob put his hands up and acted as if he wanted nothing to do with the argument.

"Leave me out of this. I don't care how much money they have given me to handle. I am not converting." Jacob walked with his cane down the hall. "I am going home away from all this madness. Did I tell you I get to travel to Israel in the Pope's own jet?" He waved and walked off.

"I haven't gotten to fly in his jet, yet!" Jean Philippe spoke to Jacob's back. The other man waved.

"He will do the foundation proud. He's gotten back something he needed, a reason to live." Abdul watched the man walk down the staircase.

"How about you?" Jean Philippe leaned against the marble railing.

"The Rector of St. Martin's and this." He pointed to his new Bishop's ring.

"And you?" Jean Philippe looked deeper into his friend's eyes.

"He didn't come to kill the Pope. Did he?" Abdul asked then leaned up against the railing also.

"No, he didn't."

"You gave the gunman the papers. Didn't you? Or at least forced Leno to do it?"

"Oui."

"Why?"

"No one needed to know the rest of the story, where the money was moved to, how it was going to be used and what we knew about them. For everyone's sake it was better that one man die quickly and that the story is buried with him."

"We still have some Cardinals and his one remaining assistant priest who knows."

"It would appear that the involved Cardinals and Father Anthony have entered a cloistered monastery with a vow of silence in exchange for not undergoing civil prosecution. The rest of the people who were in that room have been sworn to secrecy by the Pope himself. All of the Conclave

SEAN DAVID MORTON - WAYNE E. HALEY

records are sealed in the archives, not to be touched for a hundred and fifty years."

"But two men died! What about the other?"

"Cleaning up a loose end."

"That's not Church business. Is this another secret?"

"Yeah, like the truffles in my safe." Jean Philippe touched his nose in an indicator of knowledge.

"Oh yeah. . . the truffles."

"That could have killed me if I had opened it. You knew that?" They started to walk down the staircase.

"But I knew you wouldn't." Abdul was laughing.

"But who the hell got it opened? That is what I want to know, in less than an hour. This guy could make a fortune. Clifford still has the offer of a bunch of money for anyone who can do that." They were now halfway down the staircase. "I have to get a hold of Father Leno and see who he used."

"He is still mad at you for the stunt of putting your friend's name on the list of people that got it. You know. . . the one you happened to kill."

"Could be. . . probably. . . but there is still a lot of money to get from the Clifford Safe Company once we have proven to them that their safes are not impregnable." They were walking across St. Peter's Square in the warm Italian sunlight.

"I gave them the combination." Abdul acknowledged one of the priests that were passing.

"You gave them the combination?!!"

"Yeah, I did."

"Wonderful! Another great deal you've ruined."

"Remember, secrets?!"

"Yeah, Yeah." They walked toward the edge of the Square looking for a place to have dinner and a glass of good wine.

The End